# THE BERLIN TRAITOR

## A.W. HAMMOND

*echo*
PUBLISHING

**echo** PUBLISHING

An imprint of Bonnier Books UK
Level 45, World Square,
680 George Street
Sydney NSW 2000
www.echopublishing.com.au

Bonnier Books UK
4th Floor, Victoria House,
Bloomsbury Square
London WC1B 4DA
www.bonnierbooks.co.uk

Copyright © A.W. Hammond 2023

All rights reserved. Echo thanks you for buying an authorised edition of this book. In doing so, you are supporting writers and enabling Echo to publish more books and foster new talent. Thank you for complying with copyright laws by not reproducing or transmitting any part of this book by any means, electronic or mechanical – including storing in a retrieval system, photocopying, recording, scanning or distributing – without our prior written permission.

Echo Publishing acknowledges the traditional custodians of Country throughout Australia. We recognise their continuing connection to land, sea and waters. We pay our respects to Elders past and present.

This is a work of fiction. Names, characters, businesses, places, events, locales and incidents are either the products of the author's imagination or used in a fictitious manner. Any resemblance to actual persons, living or dead, or actual events is purely coincidental.

First published 2023

Printed and bound in Australia by Griffin Press

The paper this book is printed on is certified against the Forest Stewardship Council® Standards. Griffin Press holds chain of custody certification SCS-COC-001185. FSC® promotes environmentally responsible, socially beneficial and economically viable management of the world's forests.

Editor: Anna Rogers
Page design and typesetting by Shaun Jury
Cover design: Debra Billson
Cover images: Ruins of the Reichstag, Berlin, Germany, 1945?, Lebrecht Music & Arts / Alamy Stock Photo; Portrait of Soviet woman officer during World War 2, Artem Gvozdkov / Alamy Stock Photo; Man in archway, Mark Owen / Trevillion Images; Vintage military motorcycle standing in a field during the reconstruction of Liberation of Gomel, Zayne C / Shutterstock

A catalogue entry for this book is available from the National Library of Australia

ISBN: 9781760687533 (paperback)
ISBN: 9781760687540 (ebook)

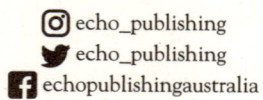

echo_publishing
echo_publishing
echopublishingaustralia

## ABOUT THE AUTHOR

A. W. Hammond was born in South Africa and emigrated to Australia as a child. He currently works at RMIT University and lives in Melbourne with his wife and daughters.

*For Berni*

*The sudden events that blind us with their light
had roots in the slowly-turning decades.*
Mick Herron, *Spook Street*

# PARIS
## Tuesday, 31 July 1945

# ONE

The man stood beside him, too close for it to be accidental, even in a crowded bar. Auguste Duchene could smell the brandy on the stranger's breath. If he was lucky, it was just a swig for confidence. If he was unlucky, the better part of the bottle. Drunk is hard to reason with, and reasoning was what he needed to do right now. Now that he had a gun held to his ribs.

He should have been paying closer attention, should have noticed them entering the small brasserie by the Bateau-Lavoir. Although it was well attended tonight, he had chosen this vantage point at the bar so he could keep an eye on the door. But he'd been a fool to let his guard down, if only for one hour, one hour in eleven months. Since Paris had been liberated from the Germans, and the rumours of his role in the city's occupation had begun, he had remained vigilant.

But he'd picked this place specifically because it was away from his new apartment, not the old one he couldn't return to. Here he was, halfway up the Butte Montmartre, two arrondissements away, at a restaurant he hadn't been to in over eight years. Not since the Paris International Exposition had sought to assure everyone of a united Europe.

All it had taken was a letter and a photograph of Marienne, only recently returned to his worn black wallet. Contact, after so many months of travelling, and the confirmation of a location – Sétif in Algeria – would have been cause for a celebration at home, but the letter contained bigger news – her return to journalism, her decision to put the war behind her and seek a new future.

'Auguste Duchene?'

The man wasn't alone. He had arrived with two others, about twenty minutes earlier. Their worn raincoats, battered caps, out of place in summer, were not uncommon for black marketeers, which is what he'd assumed they were from their furtive movements. They'd gathered at a small table and ordered only coffee – or coffee substitute. The return to civilisation was long and Paris was still troubled with food shortages. His meal had been a simple one too, moules frites and a young, acidic sauvignon blanc.

The two men at the table started to stand.

Duchene glanced at the maître d', whose attention moved elsewhere, although his brow furrowed and his eyes grew wide.

'Monsieur, we can assume your guilt from your silence and I can pull the trigger now,' said the man beside Duchene. His voice was tight and forced but betrayed his middle-class accent. His shirt had worn cuffs and the skin on his ring finger was pale from a missing wedding band.

'Witnesses?'

'They will understand.'

'And the owner? His restaurant will now be the site of a murder.'

'An execution.'

The pain was shocking, almost overwhelming, as the man brought the back of the gun up against the side of Duchene's head. It flooded across his forehead as blood ran down his face. He began to fall, grabbing the bar stool so he wouldn't land on his back. But he'd only slowed his fall. In a moment the man planted a foot on his chest and completed Duchene's journey to the floor.

The restaurant erupted into noise and movement. Some diners headed for the door while others stood to get a better view, their faces distorted with fear or excitement.

The maître d' was out from behind the bar. Dropping his charade of ignorance, he helped the man to haul Duchene to his feet. 'Apologies, all. No harm done. Too much to drink. Please return to your seats and I'll refill your glasses. On the house.'

Were his head not spinning, Duchene would have been impressed by the speed with which the maître d' had sought to secure the night's takings.

'This way,' he said in softer tones to the man with the gun, gesturing with his head towards the kitchen door.

As Duchene was dragged into the kitchen, a ruddy cook shouted, 'Trouble?' without looking up from the filet he was searing.

'I have it under control,' the maître d' snapped.

Duchene tore an arm free and grabbed for a pan. The maître d' shrieked and recoiled, but the blow never landed. One of the men behind Duchene bludgeoned the back of his arm with a heavy cosh and a new pain raced through his bones.

The pan clattered onto the floor, the cook swore and an apprentice scrambled to retrieve it. Moments later, Duchene was out into the warm night air, sprawled on the cobblestones where the men had thrown him.

Knee on Duchene's chest, rough hands pulling through his pockets, the maître d' seized the wallet and pulled out its few notes. Far from a fortune but more than the cost of his meal.

He slapped Duchene across the face. 'Bring trouble into my restaurant?'

'Them. Not me.'

'No. *You*, Monsieur Duchene. There are those of us who know what you did. Not many, but just enough to make it right.'

He got up and nodded to the other men. 'Away from here, so the customers don't hear the noise.'

For the third time this evening Duchene was hauled to his feet. But this time they knew better. Following the initiative of the maître d', they patted him down, removed the knife from his boot and tied his hands with his own belt. Then they marched him deeper into the darkness, away from the lights of Boulevard de Clichy and its dance halls and cabarets.

The adrenaline spike had been replaced by a growing chill through his hands and his face. For a moment it seemed he was outside his body, watching himself being led through a grimy alleyway with, at the end, an unparalleled view of the City of Lights. From up on the hill, the grandeur of Paris so easily cancelled out the struggle of the day to day – the ration lines, the new graves, the shorn women, the returned prisoners with their haunted eyes.

Confused and desperate, he started to shudder from the pain. 'What is it you think I've done?'

'Think?' said the man with the gun. 'We know.'

'I can't plead my case?'

'We're not without mercy. Pleading won't make this quick.'

'Good to know you have my best interests in mind.'

This was no justice. It was gossip and rumour dressed up as evidence. Likely they had done things to survive, and had compromised themselves.

His fear was becoming anger, and this was a good thing. Anger could be a weapon.

'Your wife,' Duchene said.

The man stopped for a moment.

'Your wife. She left while you were fighting for France?'

'What?'

He had to get him talking, distract him, find an opportunity.

'The pistol you're holding. It's a Free French service revolver, supplied by the Americans. You were in England with de Gaulle. You fought to liberate France after Normandy.'

'So?'

'The pale stripe on your finger. You used to wear a wedding band. You don't anymore.'

'She could have died.'

'Perhaps, but then you'd probably still wear it – in her memory.'

'Shut up. Want me to shoot you here?' The man raised his voice. A moment later a light in a ground-floor apartment went on.

Duchene stopped walking. 'You know this isn't the same. Killing unarmed Frenchmen isn't the same as killing Nazis.'

'You're a collaborator.'

'Are you sure? Why not round up the maître d'? He would have served German soldiers as they strolled around the Butte.

He made money from them, fed them and chose not to poison the first one who crossed his door.'

'That's different.'

'It's complicated. And it was complicated for me too. Killing me won't bring her back to you.'

'Shut up.'

At an apartment up ahead, the back door opened and an old man in threadbare slippers stuck his head out. He held an ornate walking stick.

'I'm sorry. She shouldn't have treated you that way,' Duchene continued.

'Quiet!'

Duchene could feel the blood on his face, sticky now.

The old man looked them up and down.

'Go back inside,' said the gunman. 'You need to go back inside.'

The old man's grip on the stick tightened.

'Not out here,' he said. 'I've seen the bodies in the streets. You just leave them for the rats and dogs. You never clean up after yourselves.'

The gunman shook his head. 'It's a warning to others.'

'It's a disgrace. We're not the Germans. We're French. We respect the dead. *Our* dead.'

'Get back in –'

Duchene rushed forward, driving his legs so hard that his feet stung as they slapped on the cobblestones. His instinct was to close his eyes, waiting for the shot, but somehow, with his hands bound in front of him, he needed to steer his course right. If he fell, he wouldn't be getting up again.

The old man reached for his door handle, but with the stick

in his hand, the movement was awkward and slow. This gave Duchene the necessary seconds to hurl himself, shoulder first, through the doorway and into the old man, who toppled to the floor. An instant later, he let go of any guilt as a shot splintered the doorframe. Duchene's heavy-handedness had been justified. The old man might be bruised but he wasn't shot. With a kick, Duchene slammed the door shut and hit the hallway light switch with his arm.

The darkness wasn't absolute but it was something.

As he bent low to grab the cane in both hands, Duchene felt a sharp pain in his back as his body rebelled against the sudden movement. Putting the walking stick between his knees, he slid its metal tip between the belt and his wrists. Just as he loosened the knot, there was a smashing of glass behind him.

By now the old man had hauled himself up and was leaning against the wall. 'Fuck off. All of you!' he shouted.

Duchene, more than happy to obey, threw the front door open and ran out into the street, clutching the walking stick. Hoping instinct would guide him, he turned right, before reaching a narrow set of stairs that cut between two terraces and down to brighter streets below. With one hand on the central railing that divided the steps, Duchene risked taking them two at a time. He could hear the shouts of the men echoing through the canyons of buildings around him. As he slowed to risk a glance over his shoulder, he saw only a few night-time strollers.

When he reached a wider, well-lit street, he stopped briefly to draw breaths of relief into his lungs, then ran on. His legs were burning, his vision blurring, his back jarring with every foot pound on the street – but he was alive.

# Wednesday, 1 August 1945

# TWO

It had been a disturbed night. The pain in his head had spurred him to consciousness, fighting the fatigue that tried to drag him back to slumber. He had remained in a state of suspension, too weary to get up, too sore to find proper sleep. There were moments where he must have passed out, however, moments that brought strange dreams.

Marienne was just ahead of him, winding her way through an Algerian souk where narrow lanes and rippling shade cloths cast dark shadows under the desert sun. Instead of colourful spices, grey ash and dust spilled from baskets and pots. What should have been vivid silks were little more than mouldy shrouds. Occasionally, Marienne, her face full of fear, would look over her shoulder to something behind him. As is the way of dreams, he didn't have full control over his body and however much he tried, he couldn't turn his head to see who was pursuing him, but he knew what they were – creatures of myth, things from the grave, ghouls who did not take kindly to the French occupying their lands.

Too early in the morning, he rose and splashed water on his face. The wound on his head was still an angry red. But, given how he looked, it could pass for the result of a moment of aging clumsiness rather than a cause for suspicion.

The apartment was still dark, still unfamiliar, even though he'd spent six months hiding out here. It consisted of a living room, bedroom and small kitchen. What limited wall space it had was covered with cabinets and cupboards, which had once held a healthy inventory of life's necessities recast in their wartime roles as luxury items. The apartment had once belonged to a friend, who'd managed to scavenge enough to trade and trade enough to set up a healthy black-market business while the Germans were in the city. But, like so many, he hadn't survived the war.

The dreams from last night still fresh in his mind, Duchene dressed, then, after using the grounds from yesterday's coffee to brew a weaker iteration, rummaged in his wallet for the letter from Marienne and the photo it contained. He had taken it yesterday from the letterbox at his old apartment building which, thanks to an irregular mail service, and no remaining friends, was often empty. There had been two other items: a plain brown envelope with a typewritten address and a pornographic postcard, on the back of which was written a profanity-riddled death threat. After his experience last night, abusive smut was the least of his problems.

As he sipped his coffee, which managed to be both weak and bitter at the same time, he re-examined the photo for signs that Marienne was alright. She was standing on the outskirts of a mud-brick town in clear sunlight, a scarf around her head and a camera around her neck. Her smile and casual stance suggested nothing but confidence and comfort. In the background he could see robed Algerian men and women apparently going about their day under the gaze of stern gendarmes with rifles. Nothing suggested she was in danger and certainly nothing suggested pursuers risen from the grave.

He removed some stale bread from the bin, picked out the mould and toasted it as he counted his cigarettes. Seven Gauloises. If he rationed them to two a day, one over morning coffee and the other after dinner, he could make it to the end of the week. To get more he would need to find something to trade, and risk possible identification.

Duchene spread a little margarine over the bread before working what remained of his rhubarb jam out of its tin. He'd scraped it so thoroughly that he was sure he'd taste aluminium on the toast, but it was preferable to mould.

With the coffee, toast and cigarette in hand, he tugged a dandelion free from his window box and dropped it in the sandy-bottomed tank he kept in the living room. A small leathery head appeared from its shell and sniffed at the offering.

While he smoked, ate and drank, he looked over the small library he'd managed to salvage from his old apartment. Only a few of his favourites had survived plunder, and what remained was an erratic collection of French classics – Dumas, Hugo and Camus – and some international works – Kafka, Joyce, Conrad. Ironically, despite their help in liberating the city, nothing by an American had survived – no Steinbeck, no Wharton and, most frustratingly of all, he had only one Hemingway left, *The Sun Also Rises*. Perhaps a love of books was something else he'd need to let go of in this new world.

As he was savouring the last of the cigarette, he heard a knock. Duchene dropped the Gauloise into an ashtray and moving as quietly as he could, the old man's walking stick in his hand, he cracked the door open so he could just see the lobby outside.

Three men in military uniforms, two French and one American. They must have slipped in while a neighbour was moving through the street door.

'Monsieur Duchene,' said the more senior of the French soldiers. A captain – young, blond, his cap already under his arm.

*Presumptuous.*

'Monsieur, we know you're at home. We'd like to talk, please.'

'What sort of talk?' Duchene asked.

'Ah, Monsieur. We have a favour to ask and…coffee. Let's make a cup and talk.'

'I also have cigarettes.' The American, a major, spoke in English.

'Cigarettes,' Duchene said as he unsnibbed the door. 'You should have started with that.'

# THREE

The youngest of the trio had produced, from a briefcase, not only an unopened can of coffee, but also a small bag of sugar, a litre of milk and, as the American had promised, three packets of Lucky Strike. These now sat on a low table in the centre of the living room, where Duchene sat in an armchair, the two senior soldiers on the settee.

This arrival at his front door was alarming. Not because they were representatives of the military, but because they had found him when he had sought not to be found. He had kept his profile low, stayed out of neighbourhoods where he was known and watched for strangers seen more than once. He wasn't prepared to be so quickly bought, but he did find his mind wandering at the prospect of a new supply of caffeine and nicotine.

'I'm Captain Henri Martin,' said the captain, in French, 'and this is Major Greer. In the kitchen is Corporal Bellerose, my orderly.'

'Good to meet you.' The American held out a sun-weathered hand. 'Are you okay?' He nodded at the plaster on Duchene's head.

'Just a bump.'

'A big one,' said Greer.

'And a cut.' Martin was looking over his shoulder into the kitchen. 'You should get someone to look at that.'

Duchene plucked a packet of cigarettes from the coffee table. The American, in fact all these men, were young for their rank – not uncommon after the war. This was to be expected for all the obvious reasons, and these days he lacked certainty when putting an age between eighteen and thirty. He considered that he knew when a man had reached forty: it showed in his face, the sense of foreboding and mortality, although that could just as easily have been the bias of his own experiences.

Duchene peeled back the foil and offered the pack to the others.

'Oh, thank you, but you enjoy those. We have our own,' Martin said, offering a Chesterfield to Greer. Now that the American's cap was off, his sharp buzz cut drew attention to a damaged left ear. There was scar tissue where a lobe should have been and more signs of injury below it on his neck.

Eventually the coffee arrived – the French press, three cups and a jug of milk. Unable to find a sugar bowl, because there wasn't one, the corporal had stuck a teaspoon directly into the bag. This seemed to bother Martin, who sent him back to find another cup as an alternative.

The absurdity of these square-shouldered, uniformed men crowded into his tiny living room did not escape Duchene.

Perhaps that was the purpose of a civilised ritual. These men had experienced the brutality of war and observing niceties underscored that it was worth it in the end. Duchene smiled to himself as the corporal served each of them.

'Merci, Bellerose.' The American was watching Duchene through narrowed eyes.

When they all had their drinks and had lit cigarettes, Bellerose passed Martin a dog-eared folder.

'Do you mind if we speak English?' the captain asked as he leafed through the pages.

Duchene nodded. The coffee was strong, reviving his senses. He glanced up at Bellerose.

'That's good,' he said in English. The corporal didn't react. 'C'est bon.'

'We're all fluent here,' Martin said.

'Not always.' Greer grinned. 'I've been known to struggle after a few whiskys.'

Martin laughed a little too loudly before addressing Duchene. 'I'm sure you're keen to know what this is all about. This is your service record.'

'You're not planning on inviting me to re-enlist, I hope?'

The men looked at one another.

'You are.'

'We'll get to that,' said Martin. 'We should start with introductions. The corporal and I are here on behalf of the French Forces in Berlin. Major Greer, as I'm sure you can tell, is American. Here on behalf of the Office of Strategic Services.'

Both Martin's and Greer's uniforms bore medals, in the former's case a Croix de Guerre and a Médaille de la France Libérée. Duchene didn't know the American's. He'd seen enough GIs in on the streets of Paris after the war to be familiar with their casual swagger and breezy confidence – they didn't carry themselves like European soldiers. But Greer had an air of measured formality.

That and his rank suggested he was a career officer, trained at a military college.

Martin gestured at the papers with his cigarette. 'Yes, we'd like to talk to you about helping your country again.'

'Not just your country, the Allies,' Greer added.

'I've had enough of the army.'

'Ah yes, you served in the Great War, were promoted to sergeant, and afterwards you taught English and German up until '42.'

'Did you ever consider staying in the military?' Major Greer asked.

Duchene took a sip from his coffee and followed it with a drag from his cigarette. 'I saw so many young men die, their lives pointlessly lost to machine-gun fire and mustard gas. I understand we won, I understand why we fought, but I struggle, still struggle, with the cost it took to get us there.'

Duchene broke the silence that followed. 'And now, again, a quarter of a century later, we're in the same place. After another war with far more deaths.'

Greer inclined his head. 'I won't tell you you're wrong. The cost was too great, far greater than it should have been. But that's exactly the reason we need to make sure it never happens again. We need to make sure the Germans stay in their place and that they're denazified. You read about Potsdam?'

'Yes,' said Duchene. 'Germany is to be divided into occupation zones.'

'Not just Germany, Berlin,' said Greer. 'Which is why we're here.'

Martin was quick to speak. 'We need your help in Berlin.'

'Help?'

'We'd like you to re-enlist and yes, help us find someone. We understand you've helped to locate missing people in the past.'

'That was in Paris. Children mostly, during the war. I'd say it's safe to assume this hasn't got anything to do with that.'

Greer held up his hand. 'We can't go into details now – you'd be properly briefed in Berlin – but your personal experience is required to find this person. It's why we've sought you out.'

*Sought.* An interesting choice of word.

'It wasn't easy finding you. We went to your apartment,' Martin said.

'Not much left of it.' Greer had lit another cigarette, his hand cupped around the Zippo, a habit from the front line. 'The only thing still intact was your letterbox in the lobby. So we sent you a letter.'

'You did?'

'A week ago.'

Ah, the unopened brown envelope still sitting on his kitchen table. He should have spotted it, he should have known.

'I only just collected it yesterday. I'm sorry, I haven't had a chance to read it.'

'It's no trouble. We've found you now.'

Except it was trouble. For him. Because someone had been watching the box and had followed him, someone working for Greer. And he should have spotted the tail.

'We need your help to stop another war from happening,' said Greer.

'You're talking about Stalin.'

'We are.'

'I thought the Soviets were our allies.'

'We had the same enemy, but it's not quite the same thing. Now that the fascists have been dealt with, it's back to taking a hard look at the communists.'

If it had taken a globe-spanning war to 'deal with' the fascists, Duchene didn't want to imagine what it would take to bring an end to communism.

'Your wife,' said Greer, 'she was a communist?'

'You've done some digging. She was. Is she still? Who knows? I don't even know if she's still alive. We haven't spoken in eight years. I believe she got out of Spain. That's what her last letter said. After that there was no contact.'

'But you never joined the PCF yourself?' Martin asked.

'The French Communist Party? No. I was a teacher. I was responsible for the manipulation of young minds. I wasn't interested in being subjected to it myself.'

Martin smiled, then leant forward, elbows on his knees. 'If you felt this way, why didn't you, as her husband, compel her to resign?'

'If you met her, you'd understand. What's my wife got to do with this? You already know I'm not a communist and that I had my daughter to raise.'

'Marienne,' Greer said. 'Fought in the liberation of Paris, then joined the French Forces of the Interior under Colonel Rol, also a communist.'

'It is possible to be French, a communist and a patriot. I believe that's how Rol would describe himself. But for Marienne, it was more about fighting Germans than it was about ideology. Your concern about communists seems rather extreme?'

'They've held onto Poland, held onto all the territories they took from the Germans, and they've spent the better part of the last three months dismantling what was left of German munitions factories and hunting for weapons engineers to ship back home. The fear is justified.'

Duchene sighed, more loudly than he'd intended. 'Marienne isn't a communist. She's a journalist. But you've done the vetting. You wouldn't be approaching me if you were concerned about my loyalty.'

'That's true,' said Martin, 'but we wanted to hear it from you, in person.'

After a gesture from Greer, Bellerose removed some forms from his briefcase and put them on the table in front of Duchene.

'This is the offer.' The major tapped the papers. 'You sign these and we reinstate you as a sergeant in the 1st Armoured Division. Then you accompany us to Berlin. No more hunting for the next meal or lining up with a ration card – you'll start drawing a salary and you'll be eating with officers.'

'And serving your country,' Martin added.

'You forgot the part about stopping the next world war,' Duchene said.

Greer removed his hand. 'Let's take that as read.'

Martin laid a pen on the pages. 'Would you like some time to think about it? We can come back in an hour.'

Duchene looked at the forms. His date of birth, address and occupation had all been typed in. Only the final line awaited his signature and Martin's.

'I know you want a decision quickly,' Duchene said, 'but I'm afraid I'm going to have to say no.'

'Monsieur, please take the time to think about it,' Martin said.

'I don't want to re-enlist. I hope I haven't wasted your time.'

Greer held up his hand again. 'The world has changed, the circumstances have changed.'

'Being a soldier hasn't. Those circumstances have been the same for thousands of years. Soldiers are ordered to kill, and I'm done with killing.'

The major was the first to stand. He bent down and ground out his cigarette, straightened his tie and replaced his cap under his arm. Martin moved a little more slowly, watching Duchene, struggling to keep his expression impassive.

'Corporal,' he said, 'if you could?'

The young soldier put Duchene's military record and the enlistment papers back in the briefcase. Before closing it, he removed a card and passed it to Duchene.

'In case you change your mind,' said Martin.

'I won't.'

Greer was already at the door, holding it open for the other men. 'A lot of damage at your apartment – door smashed in, furniture broken, books torn to shreds. Some angry people went through there.'

'They did.'

'This is a way to put an end to that.'

Duchene had anticipated this. 'I'm quite aware of my situation, thank you.'

'It would be a failure on our part if we didn't make it clear to you. We know you looked for missing children during the war. But some of those were children of collaborators, which in turn makes your actions...'

'I choose to emphasise *children*.'

'Clearly others emphasise *collaborator*,' Greer said.

'We're limited in our influence,' Martin said. 'There's only so much we can do to make sure that the law is followed. De Gaulle does not support vigilantism. It's the people who are seeking retribution.'

'It will pass,' said Duchene.

Greer nodded at the wound on Duchene's head. 'Not fast enough, it would seem.'

'My caution has been lax. You've helped me to realise that. I won't be returning to my apartment.'

'There's nothing keeping you here,' Greer said. 'No wife. No daughter.'

Duchene looked towards the tank.

'You can't be serious. The animal comes with its own home. It's ready to move now.'

But they didn't understand. The tortoise was just a tortoise. But what the tortoise represented, that was something else.

# FOUR

It sat in the middle of the floor. It hadn't been there mere seconds ago. But now the dim lights of the living room glistened on the glass around it, while a new hole in the window brought night air into the smoke-filled space. Such a simple thing, a brick, but its sudden arrival changed everything.

Duchene grabbed the walking stick, flicked off the lights. Just before the shattering of glass he had heard the sound of rapid footsteps. Now he heard them again, heading back down the street. He pulled back the edge of the curtain and looked outside.

Another warm summer night, not so late that there weren't strollers about, engaging in that very Parisian pastime of wandering the city without a purpose. That's how the owner of the brick had distinguished themselves – they were moving with a purpose and a destination.

There were concerned faces – people looking at the window and in the direction of the disappearing figure – but then, perhaps after some brief discussion among themselves, they decided to move on, their aimlessness interrupted with a specific intention to distance themselves from Duchene.

Within three minutes the street was empty. The adjacent

apartments, however, had sprung into life and nosy neighbours were peering across. With the lights out and curtains drawn, the broken window would be less obvious. Only the keen-eyed might spot it. Even so, Duchene did not like the attention. Which was, undoubtedly, the whole point of the brick in the first place.

Letting the curtain fall closed, Duchene crossed the living room to the bedroom and picked up the trench torch he kept on the bedside table.

Most of the glass had been caught by the curtain and only a few stray shards had made it to the centre of the room. The missile had taken a chunk out of the coffee table before hitting the rug. Tied twine held a folded piece of paper to the brick. Duchene didn't need to read it to know what it said, but he went through the motions. One word: collaborator.

Perhaps he had finally been discovered, independently of last night's attempted execution. He, a self-taught investigator, had already failed to notice being followed from his old apartment by a trained tracker, so it was entirely possible that others had slipped past his guard.

But there was an even more troubling possibility. What if this was the work of Greer and Martin, using the same invisible tracker? If this was the case, it was worse – it showed that they were prepared to force his hand. A brick through a window might only be the start. What next – paint daubed on his door? It was only a matter of time before people got to talking and talk brought with it his executioners. It might not even take that. There were plenty of cases across the city where innocents had been dragged out – the men shot, the women shorn – on a mere accusation. Mob justice didn't wait for charges to be read and evidence presented.

His anonymity was being peeled away; his discovery was days, maybe hours, away. He could leave for another city, seek work as a teacher, but that would mean revisiting the ghosts of the past. Even now, sense memories would return if he passed a school – the smell of brick dust, the ringing in his ears, the taste of blood in his mouth. He could hardly imagine what it would be like to actually enter a classroom.

Duchene opened one of the large cupboards. Its stockpile had been greatly reduced, but it did contain one remaining bottle of whisky. He poured himself two fingers and as he soon as he swallowed the amber liquid, he could feel his heart slow. He hadn't registered that it was racing. He sipped again and pulled out a cigarette. The smoke and the drink would aid his calculations or, at the very least, make the difficult decisions easier.

Paris was his city. It was full of bad memories, but also good ones. Many of these occurred to him only when he was walking its streets: turning a corner to find a fountain that Marienne had paddled in when she was a toddler; stepping into a basement bar where he had taken Sabine when they were first courting. At these moments a clarity would come to him, and he could instantly return to those moments and recall his joy and excitement. These places, this city, anchored him to the past and helped him to make sense of his life and yet perhaps they were holding him in place when those he loved had gone away – Marienne to Africa, Sabine to Spain. Perhaps, it slowly dawned on him, he should move on too.

Duchene put on his hat, grasped the walking stick and picked up Captain Martin's card from the coffee table. They may have forced his hand but he had something they needed. He stepped out into the apartment foyer and, with his eyes fixed on the front door, dialled the number.

Although it was after 10 p.m., the phone was answered almost immediately, which confirmed all his suspicions.

'Captain Henri Martin's office.'

'Bellerose, let me talk to the captain. I'm in, but I have one condition.'

# PARIS
## Thursday, 12 November 1936

# FIVE

They had not expected to see a body in the Seine. But the same heavy rain that had made canals of streets and waterfalls of balconies had pulled the corpse down the river. It was late afternoon and Duchene was walking to the Châtelet Métro, with Marienne skipping ahead of him. As they crossed the Pont Neuf bridge, his ten-year-old's attention had been drawn to the activity of the police on the bank. Her laugh of damp delight had stopped, and only when Duchene caught up to her did he learn the reason.

From the bridge they could see two policemen with a tarpaulin struggling to shield the victim from prying eyes. In the dim light, it was hard to make out details, but there seemed to be enough flesh still left on the face to make it unlikely that the body had been in the river for too long. There were eels in the Seine that would make quick work of soft flesh.

'Is he dead?' Marienne asked.

'I'm afraid so. We should keep moving.'

'I'd like to watch.'

'It doesn't upset you?'

'No. I didn't know him. And everyone dies, eventually.'

These occasional, matter-of-fact observations made him love

her all the more. Like a small adult, who'd already seen enough of the world to be at peace with its casual indifference.

'How did he die?' she asked.

'I can't see. He could have drowned.'

'Could he have killed himself?'

'Maybe. It might be reported in the papers.'

'Why wouldn't they report it?'

'Because not every death is newsworthy. People often die in the Seine. Or their bodies are thrown into it.'

'He could have been murdered,' said Marienne. 'There will be evidence. Wounds. Clues. A note.'

The police had now covered the corpse with the tarpaulin, observed by onlookers from the Quai de la Mégisserie who were braving the rain to look down on the proceedings. One of the policemen, a large man with a walrus moustache, waved them off.

Duchene placed a hand on Marienne's shoulder. 'Come on, Poirot, let's go.'

Although the rain was easing, they resumed their brisk pace across the bridge.

'Poirot would find a solution in an instant,' Marienne said.

'Let's continue in English.'

She changed language and repeated herself.

'Good. Poirot is a terrible stereotype.'

'Hey, no French.'

'Stereotype is also an English word. They learnt it from us.'

'Well, Poirot is not French.'

'I know. But I knew a few Belgians and they were nothing like him.'

'In the war?'

'Yes,' he replied. 'I love that you love reading, but does it have to be Agatha Christie?'

'Lots of people read her.'

'Yes, but popular does not always mean good.'

They reached the Métro entrance, with its Art Nouveau roof of green iron and frosted glass, then descended the narrow stairs into the warren of humid tunnels and platforms. Marienne, born a Parisian, moved with confidence, navigating her way to the right line.

As they stood on the platform, she took the book they had bought out of its paper bag – *Murder in Mesopotamia* by Agatha Christie. Marienne pored over the cover, which featured a clear sky above an archaeological dig filled with turbaned workers. In the background was a river, the Euphrates or the Tigris, undoubtedly, and cruising its waters was a boat with a triangular sail.

Duchenne tapped the boat without speaking.

Ever the teacher's daughter, Marienne answered immediately, her eyes alight. 'It's called a felucca. They have them in Egypt as well.'

'A felucca,' he repeated.

He liked the bookshop, although it was some distance away. Its light-filled space, almost completely given over to shelves, included a mezzanine level, with a low roof and a spiral staircase that rattled as you ascended. As a small child Marienne had loved climbing it, and it continued to enchant her. The shop had a well-put-together collection of foreign language books – English titles mostly, but a good selection of Arabic and Italian. There were German and Spanish books too, though in the last three years Duchene had noticed that they were seldom restocked and new works were rare. Change, he thought, is not always good for creativity.

On the Métro Marienne started to work through the English of her new acquisition. He reached into his brown bag for the treasure he'd allowed himself: a copy of the American magazine *Esquire*, containing a long story called 'The Snows of Kilimanjaro' by Ernest Hemingway.

Marienne smiled up at him as they travelled onwards below the city.

❧

The rain had stopped falling by the time they had emerged from the underground and started the short walk towards their apartment in Saint-Ambroise. He hadn't always lived here, but had moved because the local school was a good one. It did mean a long journey to work for Sabine and him, but Marienne's grades and enthusiasm for her education justified it.

Duchene hadn't finished the Hemingway – it had been a mistake to start reading – and planned to do so as soon as dinner was done and Marienne in bed, though Sabine would want to talk about the day. He would need patience. He might like to see Africa, or the Tigris or the Euphrates. Just for a time. A little hardship to stoke his love of cities.

A cry pulled him back into the world.

Marienne, who had been balancing beside him along the raised stone edging of a garden bed, footsure, her arms held out like a tightrope walker, now lay on top of some pale yellow dahlias. She was already starting to stand, but she had cut her knee.

He could feel the warmth rush to his face so suddenly that it prickled the skin. He quickly knelt beside her. 'Are you alright?'

She was staring at the blood that was starting to well.

'Marienne?'

Her face serene, she pressed the edges of the wound, forcing out some more of the crimson fluid.

Shifting his satchel, Duchene searched his pockets for a handkerchief but Marienne had already found her own and was staunching the flow.

'Let me get another one.' He tried another pocket.

'Papa, I'm fine.' She stepped off the crushed flowers and back onto the pavement.

'Are you sure? Do you want me to carry your bag?'

'Papa.'

Her tone told him that was the end of it. With the same calmness that had descended on her in the flowerbed she resumed walking towards their apartment.

---

Sabine was not home. She was often late, either working a late shift or attending party meetings. He lit the gas and put the kettle on to boil before looking in the bathroom cabinet. He found a tin of adhesive plasters, but it was empty.

'We're out of plasters. I'll go and ask Camille, then I'll make you something hot to drink. Chocolate?'

'I'd prefer tea,' she said. 'I'm not a baby.'

He'd misplayed that one. He'd thought the extravagance of offering what little drinking chocolate they had left would be appreciated. Unlike her parents, Marienne was insulated for the most part from the depression, but even today's little journey, with its Métro tickets and expensive foreign books, would need to be accounted for. He and Sabine would have to monitor their finances for the rest of the month.

After crossing the narrow corridor that separated their apartment from Camille's, Duchene knocked lightly on her door. He could hear the sound of a piano being averagely played. It couldn't be Camille, so she must be teaching. He knocked more loudly.

Camille was closer to his own age than Sabine. On more than one occasion, as they walked with Marienne through the streets, they had been mistaken for husband and wife. Perfume wafted towards him as she opened the door and frowned at him from beneath her black bob.

'Auguste, I have a lesson.'

'I know. Sorry. I was just wondering if you had a spare plaster, maybe two? Marienne fell and cut her knee.'

The frown lifted. 'She's alright?'

'Surprisingly.'

'Hold on. I have a new tin. When you have a chance, you can replace it.'

The reheated boeuf bourguignon that he and Marienne ate later, served with the remainder of that morning's baguette, was another extravagance. The stove had warmed the apartment which, simple as it was, had been a lucky find. Though larger than most, with two bedrooms, a bathroom and a kitchen opening into the living room, it was, at times, a little cosy for the three of them, but with the city on their doorstep they could spend as much time outdoors as in.

After dinner, when Marienne was in her room, Duchene allowed himself the treat of a cigarette while he did the dishes. He was just placing them on the rack when he heard the front door open.

Sabine was still wearing her coat and her dark hair was damp with misting rain. Even now, in late autumn, her olive skin held the memory of the sun. Her cool blue eyes, usually so welcoming, were filled with concern.

'I know I'm late. Not a good day.'

'I'm sorry to hear that.'

'How's Marienne?'

'She cut her knee, but she's fine.'

Sabine dropped her coat onto the settee before going into Marienne's room. He could hear the murmur of their talk as he relit the stove to warm the food he had kept and poured two glasses of wine, which he set on the table. He added the ashtray from the coffee table, along with the apartment's lighter and his battered packet of Gauloises.

Eventually the door opened and he could see Marienne in bed, smiling at him.

'Goodnight,' she called.

'I love you,' he replied.

'Thank you for dinner,' said Sabine, as he put the meal before her.

'Thank you for making it.'

'She's fine?'

'She's fine.'

'And you?'

Sabine shook her head. 'No. There was a murder last night, the body thrown in the river. I knew him.'

# SIX

Duchene poured Sabine a second glass of wine. She had only picked at the food; her mind was elsewhere. As he depressed the lever on the cigarette lighter, the curved silver surface distorted his reflected face so that his eyes seemed huge.

As he sat back into his chair, he said, 'Marienne and I saw them pulling his body out of the Seine. Were you close?'

'Not close. No. His name was Marcus Vincent – he led a centrist faction in the party. He wasn't completely opposed to us, but not an ally either. Most importantly, he sat on the Central Committee. I met him a few times because of the fundraising.'

'Are you alright?'

'I'm fine. There was a meeting this evening, when news got out. They're convening the committee tomorrow. They'll need to take an extraordinary vote for someone to act as replacement. We only just had the national congress in August, so he hasn't been in the role for very long.'

Duchene sipped his wine, the note of heavy plum competing to assert itself against the taste of tobacco. Sabine prodded at the meat with her fork.

'How do you know it's a murder?' he asked.

'They've already sent police to interview some of the leadership.'

'The police identified him immediately?'

'I believe so. I heard that they didn't deliver the news with any compassion.'

'That's the Paris police for you. I doubt they'd deliver bad news to their own mothers with any sensitivity.'

'Exactly. We're not expecting much from the official investigation, Vincent being a card-carrying communist. In fact, that's probably how they identified his body.'

'You're not normally at party headquarters?'

'I was there because of my fundraising for the International Brigades. I handed over the latest donations yesterday and a few of the Central Committee members invited me back to pass on their thanks.'

'You were on the street with all that money?'

'I wasn't alone. Hugo was with me, and some of his steel workers.'

'Hugo Bloyer.'

'Of course.'

For the most part, the many party names and stories blurred and shifted in his consciousness, but Hugo Bloyer never passed without note. It wasn't his actions – he sounded like any other union leader and PCF member and his rise through the ranks clearly showed some savvy – but the fact that often, when Sabine mentioned him, she would smile.

'Why do they think it's a murder?'

Sabine put down the fork and pushed the meal to one side. 'He'd been stabbed.'

'Before he went into the river?' said Duchene, without thinking.

'Harder to do it the other way around, but not impossible, I guess.'

'I see you've got your humour back.'

She smiled. 'I've offered to help them find out what happened.'

'They don't trust the police?' Duchene asked.

'Well, they don't much care for communists.'

'You'll probably want to look at Vincent's movements on the night he died. The last person who saw him. It's obvious, but it works.'

'Well,' Sabine said, 'I did want to speak to you about that. I was hoping you might help me to discover why he was killed.'

'Help?'

'Yes.'

'I'm not sure if I can do that. The police may lack tact, but this is their job. I'm just an amateur.'

'They won't take it seriously. They were laughing on their way out the door.'

Duchene shrugged. 'I'm not sure what help I'd be.'

'You notice things. Please, Auguste. You've helped us before, when Le Blanc disappeared.'

'I was helping you, not the party. And only because a mother and her children were going to be left destitute.'

She reached out across the table and held both his hands in hers. 'Please. For me.'

'And the Central Committee has agreed to this?'

'Not yet. I haven't asked them.'

## Friday, 13 November 1936

# SEVEN

The autumn wind brought with it ice and leaves. It was strange to see their brown and orange shapes in the heart of the city, so far away from the large gardens and cemeteries. Duchene was struggling to keep his hat on as he walked arm in arm with Sabine up Rue La Fayette. As a new blast pulled at his coat, Duchene felt her press herself tightly against him. Two blocks ahead lay the headquarters for the French section of the Communist International or the PCF, depending on your point of view.

'It's going well, by the way. Really well,' Sabine said from just below his shoulder.

'What's that?'

'The fundraising. We've brought in fifteen thousand francs so far.'

'That's impressive. Perhaps a new job for you?'

'What would that be?'

'Not a *saleswoman*, obviously. That would make you part of institutions designed to exploit the working class.'

'Glad to see you're learning.'

A bus rumbled in front of them at an intersection, its blue

headlamps casting a spectral light across the puddles on the road ahead. The passengers huddled on the platform at the back were rugged up, their pale faces tight as they braced themselves against the force of the wind.

'It was worth it,' Sabine said. 'It was a lot of work but it was worth it. We're having success in Spain – we've joined up with the Republicans and are almost in Madrid. It shows that the world won't stand for fascists.'

'Well…fascists in Spain.'

She let go of his arm. 'That's a bit cynical.'

'I'm sorry, but I don't believe there's any glory in war. It's a myth. If you want to talk about exploiting the workers…'

'Exactly. But the International Brigades are made up of volunteers who have chosen to fight. Not conscripts.'

'They're still soldiers, fighting, dying and killing for kings and presidents.'

'Be careful, you're sounding like a seditionist.' She smiled before taking his arm once more. 'I agree it's not simple, but you've seen how willing the right are to use violence to drive their ideology. We have to be willing to do the same. We'd prefer not to, but they're intent on the death of freedom. This is a fight to defend democracy against fascist dictatorship. You've seen how Hitler seized power. Mussolini. This is why Europe needs to be vigilant.'

'Sure, but these are problems for Spain, Germany and Italy.'

Sabine stopped walking and turned to face him. 'But for how long? I'm serious about this.'

'I know you are. Your passion is just one of the things I love about you.'

'I mean I'm serious about Spain.' She lowered her voice. 'I'm thinking of joining a brigade.'

He felt his stomach drop. 'That's a war you're talking about fighting in. You could die.'

'I know.'

'What about Marienne and me?'

Sabine's eyes widened. 'It's for Marienne and you that I need to do this. Can't you see? The world is shifting around us. We're on the brink.'

'We're fine. Spain will consume itself. Germany will do the same.'

She smiled at him, her face full of warmth, free of anger. She knew exactly how to placate him and he felt torn in one direction by her appreciation and in the other by the feeling that he was being patronised.

'Auguste, you're letting your own past cloud your judgement. You've seen what war can do, so you'll do anything, even refusing to see what's happening around you, to prevent its return.'

'Perhaps I'm trying to be optimistic. But it's not a hypothetical question for me. I know what it is to feel so empty, so ground down by the death around you, that you don't even know your own self…'

'I understand. We can talk about it later. Properly.' She placed a hand on his face, her fingers like icicles along his cheek. 'I love you.'

But within him he already knew that she had made up her mind and that the purpose of their conversations would be to steer him towards a conclusion she'd already arrived at. He knew he should focus on cherishing what moments they had, but it was hard to push his resentment aside.

He sighed and put his hand over hers. 'Let's go and meet your party then.'

---

The four-storey building was pressed in on two sides but, unlike its neighbours, its ground floor was not a shop front. When Duchene had last been here, during the election, the large, flat façade had been used as a giant billboard, covered with bold political messages – 'To save France from misery and ruin the rich must pay!' – and promises of employment for civil servants, war veterans and victims, small farmers and investors. They had helped PCF representatives, as part of the Popular Front, to victory in May. Three months later, and these messages had been painted over, leaving only the words 'Parti Communiste Français' beneath two rounded pediments, each bearing a hammer and sickle painted in gold on a red background.

It was humid inside, the stuffiness made worse by so many bodies. Men in caps and berets hurried up and down the staircase, stopping only to lean into offices to exchange information. There was mould on the walls and cigarette ash on the floors and many of the lights needed replacing.

'We'll be moving offices soon,' Sabine said as she pushed her way into the reception area, where a huddle of men and women were working at a printing press. While a new block was being inked, a thin young man stood on a chair and read aloud from a notebook.

'We must remain vigilant against Trotsky and Zinoviev and their gang of counter-revolutionaries. They are assassins, as proven by the Supreme Court in Moscow. They murdered Comrade Kirov and attempted to take the life of Comrade Stalin. The Trotsky-Zinovievites are not the old guard. The old guard is Stalin. It is Molotov, Voroshilov, Kalinin and Ordzhonikidze.'

'Don't forget Kaganovich,' said an older man in spectacles.

'The Old Guard is Stalin. It is Molotov, Voroshilov, Kalinin, Ordzhonikidze and…Kaganovich. It is the people of the USSR. And we, the Communist International, support them.'

The men and women at the press briefly applauded.

'Thank you for your help, comrades.' The man climbed down from the chair.

Sabine held up her red card. 'I'm looking for Comrade Bloyer.'

'Back room,' said a tall woman who was supervising the press.

Duchene removed his hat and followed Sabine through the corridors. Cigarette smoke drifted towards them as they neared the sound of heated discussion coming from behind a closed door.

Sabine knocked loudly as she entered and the conversation was replaced with silence and hard stares. Five men were standing around a table strewn with papers and a map of Paris. One man, dark haired with heavy brows, scooped the papers into a box, while another placed his hand over a section of the map, but not before Duchene had seen that it included the Pont Neuf.

A sixth man, who was leaning against a filing cabinet, glanced up, his deep thought seemingly broken by the sudden silence. Tight curls surrounded a widow's peak that drew attention to his wide brow and sharp eyes. He smiled as he saw Sabine. His sleeves were rolled up, revealing strong arms that reached out in welcome.

'Comrade Duchene. Sabine!'

*Bloyer.*

'Comrades, you know my counterpart from the General Confederation of Labour? A forewoman from the Quai de Javel Citroën factory.' His voice was like his smile, warm and generous. He kissed Sabine on both cheeks.

A short bald man nodded. 'Your fundraising success for the International Brigades is impressive.'

'This is my husband –'

'Auguste.' Bloyer stepped forward to shake Duchene's hand. 'An honour. I have heard much about you.' He turned to the others. 'This man is a teacher, languages, at a school in the sixteenth arrondissement.'

There were nods of approval in the room, though some faces remained suspicious.

'We're here to talk with the Central Committee,' Sabine said.

'Then it's good we spoke first. We've been convened as a subcommittee to collate what information we have,' Bloyer replied.

'I was hoping to ask if Auguste could talk to the leadership,' Sabine said. 'I think he can be help us to find out what really happened.'

'Respectfully, Comrade Duchene, your husband isn't even a member of the party,' the bald man said. 'This is a particularly sensitive matter and should be handled internally.'

'I'd be happy to agree,' Duchene replied.

'There might be something to it,' Bloyer said. 'A new perspective. Someone who doesn't immediately provoke the fear of radical Bolshevism.'

Some of the men laughed.

'Besides, it's not for us to decide. Let's leave that to the wisdom of our Central Committee.' He checked his watch. 'It's almost six. Let's take our findings to them, shall we?'

'And where is the Central Committee?' Duchene whispered to Sabine.

'The top. Main meeting room.'

They gathered more party members, on each level, as they ascended towards the fourth floor, which was a mirror of those below it – narrow corridors, frayed wallpaper, small offices. When Bloyer, Sabine and Duchene first entered the meeting room, reverence and apprehension seemed to hang in the air. The conversation was quieter and the glances more furtive. But the noise soon swelled as the throng behind them arrived.

Seated at a long table was an assortment of men, from greying intellectuals to vigorous union leaders, all repositioning themselves into commendable postures of considered introspection or alert readiness. On one wall were photographs of communist luminaries, the grim beards of Marx and Engels giving way to the groomed moustaches of Lenin and Stalin. On the opposite wall were smaller framed photos of a succession of PCF leaders, ending with Maurice Thorez.

Bloyer and the bald man made their way to one side of the table and stood beside a small, well-kept man with half-glasses and closely cut greying hair. This, presumably, was the chairman. Duchene and Sabine, on the opposite side of the table, were pushed together by the crowd. Sabine gripped the tips of his fingers, her eyes wide with excitement.

The chairman hammered a worn gavel on its block. 'Comrades,

please. You are here as party members to observe this meeting, but we must be able to hear one another speak.'

'Comrade Langlois,' Bloyer said, 'before we present the subcommittee's findings, I'd like to draw your attention to an observer and minute him to the meeting. Monsieur Auguste Duchene. Husband to Comrade Sabine Duchene.'

One of the old intellectuals spoke. 'Does Comrade Duchene require an escort to these meetings? Why is he here?'

The crowd chuckled and murmured.

'Comrade Bigarde, clearly your reputation with the ladies precedes you. My husband has come to see who the competition is,' Sabine replied.

The crowd broke into laughter as Bigarde puffed and flapped his hands. The gavel came down again.

'Comrades, please, we're here to discuss the unfortunate death of Comrade Vincent and determine two courses of action: who should act as replacement until we can convene a full party vote, and, given the lack of police interest, what we should do about his death.'

'Apologies, Comrade Langlois,' Sabine said. 'Auguste is here because he might be able to help with the second matter.'

'Yes, comrade,' Bloyer said. 'He has successfully assisted the General Confederation of Labour with a private investigation before. Comrade Duchene and I believe that he might be able to assist us.'

'Very well. Welcome, Monsieur Duchene. Now to our first item. The Central Committee can vote to fill an empty position until a party congress can be convened. General Secretary Thorez is unable to make it tonight, as are Comrades Cardin, Saint-Pierre and Guernier, but we still have a quorum. As a result of the sad passing of Comrade Vincent, we will take nominations for the acting position of Central Committee member. Does anyone have a nomination?'

Bloyer broke the silence. 'I nominate Comrade Duchene.'

All eyes turned to Sabine and a murmur spread through the room and into the corridor. She let go of Duchene's hand and glanced at him, confused. There was an angle here, Duchene was sure of it. Some theatre or larger strategy at play.

'Seconded,' said the tall woman from the printing press.

'Do we have any other nominations?' Langlois asked.

The short bald man said, 'Comrade Bloyer.'

There it is, Duchene thought. A generous leader, a man who places the benefit of the collective before his and does not seek the role himself. Sabine was an offering to Bloyer's own generosity.

'Thank you, comrades. Any further nominations?'

The chairman let the silence hold for a few more seconds than were needed.

'Excellent. By a show of hands, can the committee please vote once for either candidate. Comrade Duchene.'

There were mutterings of discomfort as the party members craned their necks forward. No one at the table raised his hand.

*Sacrifice is the right word.*

'And Comrade Bloyer?'

All those around the table raised their hands.

'It is unanimous then: Comrade Bloyer is accepted as acting committee member.'

There was polite applause. A few people, mostly women, leant over to touch Sabine on the arm. She smiled and mouthed her gratitude but Duchene knew she must have seen the play, must be feeling used, and furious. But whatever she was experiencing was not apparent, either judiciously concealed or yet to be fully realised.

Langlois banged the gavel again.

'Comrade Bloyer, please take a seat with us at the table.'

Bloyer held up his hand. 'If I may, I'd like to present the findings of the subcommittee. It will be hard for everyone to see, but if I remain standing it might help a little.' Langlois nodded. 'The last time Comrade Vincent was seen alive by members of the party was two evenings ago, at approximately 6.35 on Wednesday 11 November. On the afternoon of Thursday 12 November the body of our much-missed comrade was taken from the Seine at the Pont Neuf. That evening a prosecutor interviewed key members of the Central Committee, including Comrades Langlois and Bigarde. We have sought to provide a buffer between the police and our members in government.

'We don't know how he came to be in the river, but presume it was an attempt to conceal his murder. He was stabbed to death, according to the police. They searched his apartment after identifying him by his red card, and found anonymous letters threatening his life. We have some similar letters that Vincent received here in the party offices.'

Bloyer turned to Duchene. 'We're all the target of fascists, Monsieur. In fact, not just us and not only in written form. Your wife, many of our members, have been abused on the street, spat at and sometimes beaten. Where we seek to unite the workers of the world, to give them bread on their tables and the ability and means to determine their own futures, the fascists seek only imperialist war.'

Duchene noted how quickly Bloyer had started to include himself in the party leadership.

'I understand. Thank you. And I assume there's a specific letter that makes you believe that its author is Vincent's killer?'

Everyone turned to face Duchene. Bloyer smiled. 'You're quite correct, Monsieur. We have a letter that speaks specifically of ending Comrade Vincent's life in the very way that we and the police suspect. I won't read it aloud out of respect for our dead comrade and his many friends here, but the language is offensive and dehumanising.'

'But you're not expecting the police to pursue it?' Duchene asked.

'Exactly,' Bloyer replied. 'As agents of the bourgeoisie, they have no interest in justice for communists.'

*Or they simply want to conclude the investigation so they can move on to the next one.*

'Thank you, Monsieur Duchene,' Langlois said. 'Is there any more you'd like to tell us, Comrade Bloyer?'

'That is the summary of what we have discovered. We will continue to examine Vincent's office for anything else that might explain what has happened. But the subcommittee could not agree on a recommendation. We require the Central Committee to make the decision on our behalf.'

'You could have made the casting vote, Comrade Bloyer,' said Bigarde.

'True, but the debate was impassioned and I felt I needed to bring it to the committee's attention. I abstained from my casting vote. One view was that the prosecutor won't accept our conclusion and that we're no better than our enemies if we resort to vigilante justice.'

There were gestures and expressions of agreement in the room.

'The other view,' Bloyer said, 'is that we need to send a message to those fascists and their kind that we won't sit by while heroes of the party are killed on the streets.'

As a cheer rose from the firebrands in the crowd, Langlois hammered again. 'Comrades, please!'

'My view is that the Central Committee doesn't need to make the decision now,' Bloyer shouted. 'You can hold off until you have more information. Information that I propose Comrade and Monsieur Duchene gather on our behalf. Because it's an internal matter, it makes sense for a representative to be involved, but we also need someone who can open doors that would otherwise be closed to the "red menace". And a married couple will not draw any unnecessary attention. It's the perfect solution.'

There was clapping throughout the room and for a few minutes pockets of conversation continued. Eventually, Langlois restored order.

'Monsieur Duchene,' Bigarde said, 'you have already shown you have an astute mind, though not so astute as to have joined our party. Are you available and willing to assist us with this inquiry?'

'I'd like to see the letter first – the one that you believe came from the killer.'

'And why is this important?' Bigarde asked.

'I always go back to the beginning. And seeing the note will help to understand if it is the fascists.'

'Why does that matter?'

'Because *if* the fascists are behind it, I don't want to be part of it. I don't want to give you a reason to seek vigilante justice. Street battles are the last thing Paris needs right now. It won't help your cause,' Duchene said. 'I've seen war and I've killed men. Both should be avoided at all costs.'

'Let me investigate then.' Sabine's voice carried across the room.

Duchene looked at her, but her eyes were locked on Langlois and Bloyer.

'I agree that street battles are a waste of effort. If you want to fight, you should join me in fighting the fascists who want to overthrow a free republic in Spain. But I would hope that, as a party, we would seek answers over ignorance. Let's not assume that Comrade Vincent was killed by fascists until we have proven it.'

There was another burst of noise from the crowd, voices in agreement and calling for action. The gavel banged once more.

Bloyer passed the letter across the table towards Duchene. 'Here. We would appreciate your insight.'

Duchene took the page and held it between himself and Sabine. He had to stand firm or risk stumbling as men and women tried to read the letter as well.

*Vincent — Die. Fucking Bolshevik pig. I see where you sleep. I know where you live. You are going to die like a pig. Knife to the throat. Cut up and gutted like a fish. Your blood will flow on the streets. We will drop you in the Seine and your body will never surface. Your family will know you are dead but never find you.*

'You got it?' Duchene asked Sabine. His question broke the silence that had fallen.

'Yes,' she said, her voice cracking.

He folded the letter and returned it to Bloyer.

'They also talk about his blood on the streets. It's not just about the Seine. Also, nothing explicitly suggests that the writer was a fascist. It could be someone else.'

'All true,' Bloyer said. 'It could certainly stand more investigation. Will you support us, Monsieur Duchene, and persist where the police will not?'

Near silence returned to the room. The collective intake and exhalation of breath was suspended. Just the almost motionless stirring of bodies so tightly packed, coats and elbows brushing against one another.

'I will,' he replied.

# Berlin
## Thursday, 2 August 1945

# EIGHT

From the air, green forests and farmland gave way to the devastation of a bombed-out Berlin. Duchene had already seen damage caused by shelling in the outlying rural areas. Farmhouses burnt down, the tops of trees shredded by blasts, roadways peppered with the wrecks of tanks and trucks – witness to temporary defensive positions where men had taken a stand against the advancing Red Army. Then had come the train yards and factories with their twisted metal and churned earth. Freight carriages toppled, long multi-storey foundries collapsed like toppled book stacks.

But none of it had prepared Duchene for Berlin itself.

Those buildings that hadn't completely disintegrated crested the debris like the tips of waves. In other places this sea of destruction was flat, calm and lifeless, where entire city blocks had been levelled. Of those structures that had survived, some looked as though they had burst, their red bricks spread around them like a ragged skirt. Others had fallen inwards, filled with debris that had crashed through floor after floor and erupted from ground-level windows and doorways.

Nearer the city centre, shells of apartments with only two or three walls remaining were white beneath a bright midday sun. No glint from glass as it had long since been shattered. They looked to Duchene like many-eyed skulls, the dark voids of their sockets staring over the devastation.

As the plane circled above the Spree before turning back towards the Tempelhof airfield, he could see the Reichstag, its dark stone pocked with bullet holes, its dome a precarious frame of blackened metal. The Brandenburg Gate, too, still stood, the sculpture of Victory and her horse-drawn chariot a buckled mess, the columns chipped and blackened. This was where the Nazis had made their last stand; on one side of the gate was a portrait of Stalin so large that he could make it out clearly from the air.

Duchene turned away from the window and felt his stomach roiling again as the plane hit turbulence, swaying and rocking from side to side.

'Do you want another one of these?' Greer shouted over the noise of the engines and leant towards him, holding out a thick paper bag.

Duchene shook his head. 'We're landing soon.'

'Definitely.' It was unclear if Greer's white smile signalled amusement or reassurance, but Duchene was both used to and no longer concerned about condescension.

He was, however, very conscious that millimetres of glass and aluminium were all that stood between him and the ground, thousands of metres below. As the plane had taken off, and now as it turned to level out and line up the runway, he felt the engines tugging at its wings – a contradiction in engineering, all that horsepower threatening to tear the thin walls of the aircraft apart.

'Used to hold my wife's hand on landing,' Greer said. 'We don't need to tell anyone if you think that would help?'

Duchene gripped the handrail above the seat, his eyes and jaw so tightly shut he couldn't respond to the major's jibe.

The plane shuddered violently, lifted off the ground as if unhappy with its previous efforts and then hit the runway a second time, knocking Duchene sideways in his seat and pushing his hip hard into the straps. The noise increased as its propellers reversed and the plane slowed, rapidly pulling Duchene in the opposite direction. He opened his eyes only when the plane started to taxi along the runway and the propellers were winding to a stop.

'It's not so bad, really,' Greer said. 'Always good to get your first flight over with.'

Duchene wasn't sure if he agreed.

'Easy to forget that you Europeans are more accustomed to trains and boats. The war will have changed some of that.'

'I think I'll stick to them a while longer,' Duchene replied.

Outside the smell of diesel and gasoline was strong as planes and trucks manoeuvred between hangars while US and British soldiers boarded buses headed for the terminal. Duchene stood by the cargo hatch.

'Just the one bag?' asked the young flight officer.

'No, that too.'

Strapped to the inside wall of the hold was a wicker picnic basket with a double-hinged lid on either side of a handle.

'Better keep an eye on that thing,' Greer said, as they crossed the concrete on their way to the terminal. 'Some of our boys might steal it for a mascot. Tank division would be keen.'

Unlike the homes and apartments across the city, the airport, with its strategic significance, was almost fully restored. Only a few bullet holes remained in the masonry and even now a small repair crew was working on a scaffold to patch them. Multiple American flags flew over the four-storey curved building, which stretched over a kilometre in a gentle arc. It included an administration complex and a series of hangars that dwarfed the planes they housed.

Duchene stared upwards as they entered the main lobby.

'I'll give the Nazis one thing – they knew how to build them impressive,' Greer said.

Rectangular columns of white marble rose between floor-to-ceiling windows that spilled light onto highly polished floors running hundreds of metres in either direction. The voices of huddles of soldiers and officials barely penetrated the immense void. The passenger hall could have easily accommodated several planes.

Air pulled at Duchene as they sped west along the highway. He held his hat on with one hand while the other gripped the door handle on the side of the jeep. The road was obviously used only by military vehicles – convoys of US trucks and other jeeps passed them, heading back towards the airport. He could see where damage from shells had been recently patched, bridges reinforced.

From the air the damage to the city had been overwhelming; on the ground it became more personal. As they swung off the main road, the jeep had to slow to navigate traffic that crawled through narrow passageways between hills of bricks and rubble.

There was dust was everywhere – in the air, on his breath, on the clothes of the women, mostly, who walked in single file alongside the moving traffic. Sometimes they came close to stepping out in front of the jeep, but moved quickly as it drove up behind them. More of these women worked in teams, standing atop the piles and passing bricks, hand to hand, to clear them, one at a time, from ruined buildings. Well dressed, in skirts and blouses, they were mopping their brows in the summer heat. Around them, children played in the rubble with crude toys made of cans and spent bullet casings.

Duchene tapped Greer on the arm. 'Don't they have overalls to wear? Trousers? Something practical?'

'They're wearing what they had on their backs when the bombing started. For most of the rubble women, that's their Sunday best. We've all got them working across the city. It's the only way to get it done – roads first, now habitable buildings.'

The driver sounded his horn at an old man leading a frail donkey along the road. On its bony back were pans, a chipped gramophone and rolled-up blankets. Flies had gathered around the animal's eyes but it didn't seem to have the energy to shake them off. As the jeep drove past, the old man blinked up at Duchene.

'The donkey's lucky it's still alive,' Greer said. 'Anything with a heartbeat that isn't human gets eaten.'

'You give them rations?'

'They have cards, of course, but I hear it's almost impossible to find enough to make up their daily allocation.'

'All those supplies at the airport?'

'For us, the Brits and you French. Don't feel sorry for the Germans. If they hadn't started a war, they'd have food to eat. Think about it like that and it won't keep you up at night.'

The jeep stopped at an intersection that returned them onto a wider stretch of road. A truck cruised past, its canvas off, young GIs clinging to its sides. In the heat, they'd removed their helmets and jackets, and unbuttoned their shirts, revealing dog tags dangling from tanned necks. They were smoking while Perry Como played from a portable transceiver.

One grinning soldier leant out as the truck passed a young German woman in a polka dot dress. She was petite, blonde, her bare calves covered in the ubiquitous dust. She was carrying a bucket of water, stepping around stray bricks so as not to spill her cargo.

'Veronika, dankeschön,' a shirtless GI called to her. 'Come, give us your water. We'll help you.'

The rest of the young men cleared a space and tapped the side of the truck for it to stop. The woman continued to walk, as though she hadn't heard.

'Come. Let us help. Veronika, dankeschön.'

She continued to struggle with the water, shaking her head. As the truck resumed its journey, the GI whistled and shouted, 'Here! Nimm das.' And tossed his half-finished packet of cigarettes to her.

The jeep pulled out around the truck, picking up speed on the concourse as it made its way towards a river. When Duchene looked back, the woman was bending down to pick up the cigarettes.

'Should have taken the lift,' Greer said.

'I think she was worried for her safety,' Duchene replied.

'Not from our boys. The Russkies, yes. But not from us.'

Even before they turned into the entrance drive, Duchene had a fair idea of what the building would look like. Regardless of nation, military bases were all much the same: intended to build the mythology of the noble warrior with their Romanesque stylings and Doric columns – honourable, determined, orderly. As the jeep slowed, Duchene could see a newly fortified entrance, its watch-house and boom gate reinforced with sandbags and tank traps. Major Greer presented his identification to a young military policeman and the boom gate was lifted. Above the portico of the imposing red-brick building, workers were removing stone letters, the exposed lighter brick still making the inscription legible: 'Leibstandarte Adolf Hitler'. The former home of the Führer's personal SS bodyguard.

When the jeep pulled up next to a short row of steps at the entrance, Greer grabbed his duffle bag and briefcase. Duchene went to follow suit, but the major said, 'Leave them', before turning to the driver. 'Wait here.'

Inside there was a buzz of activity, with military clerks and officers moving between rooms, their boots loud on the marble tiles, running papers upstairs, making radio calls. Duchene couldn't see a closed door anywhere as they strode down the corridor – perhaps it allowed the freedom of movement required to rush orders and bring in coffee. In one room, uniformed women, seated at tables arranged in a grid, were typing furiously from shorthand notes. The clatter of keyboards and the ping of carriage returns followed him and Greer to a closed door. The major tapped on one of its wooden panels. A voice from inside called, 'Come!'

Light from a large window fell on couches and armchairs arranged around a circular coffee table, inlaid with a yellow spearhead on a black background. It stood out in what otherwise looked more like a smoking room, with three walls of dark bookshelves, empty but for a few file boxes. To one side sat a large, leather-topped wooden desk with telephones, papers and a brass reading lamp. Against another wall were a humidor and a drinks cabinet.

Three uniformed men stood around the coffee table, one American, one British and one French – perfect for a newsreel or the start of a joke. Greer saluted the American, who then reached out to shake his hand.

'Major Greer, welcome back.'

He was greying, his face weathered by sun, his uniform taut across a barrel chest and firm belly. 'Welcome to Andrews Barracks, Sergeant Duchene. I'm Major General Earl Bennett of the Office of Strategic Services. Major Greer reports to me. This is Brigadier Thomas Wright from British Military Intelligence and Colonel Jean Leterrier of the 1st Armoured Division from Camp Cyclops. I understand you speak English?'

'I do,' Duchene replied, 'but I'm not a sergeant.'

'You're not?' Leterrier asked.

'It was a concession,' Greer replied, 'to secure Mr Duchene's help.'

'You have a problem with being paid in return for service to your country?' The dark-haired Colonel Leterrier would have been around the same age as Duchene. Among his medals were one from Verdun and another from the Somme, both of which Duchene had also received.

'Not at all. I'm here to help, but not to re-enlist.'

'Glad to hear it,' the general said. 'Let's sit down. Iced tea?' He made a quick call from his desk.

'Let's get straight on with it. As you've probably guessed, we're here as part of a joint operation, coordinated by ourselves, out of our zone but resourced and supported by our French and British colleagues. We're looking for an Oberführer from the Gestapo. We believe you had contact with him during the German occupation of Paris.'

The smell of dried blood, the sounds of gunshots, the sight of rooms stripped of their carpets for easy cleaning – in less than a second Duchene was back in that building on the Rue des Saussaies.

'I was arrested by the Gestapo a year ago. I was interviewed by an Oberführer.'

'We need you to find him.'

Duchene's mind touched lightly on a number of deeper questions: How could they know? Why did they think he could find him? *How* could he possibly find him?

'I'm not sure if I can help.'

'I know. We've pulled you a long way from home and we might only have a snowball's chance in hell, but it's important that we try.'

'I have questions.'

'We would expect so,' Leterrier said. 'We have questions too. Who shall start?' Without letting Duchene reply he continued, 'Do you know the name of this Oberführer?'

Leterrier paused, this time.

'I'm afraid that I don't,' Duchene said. 'And neither do you… that's why I'm here.'

The officers stared at him, unmoving.

'But I can give you a description. He was Bavarian, late sixties, around one and a half metres tall. His hair was black, probably dyed, parted to one side. Weak jaw, pale blue eyes. He wore half-glasses and a dark suit. Presumably some of these details may have changed.'

'Do you think you'd recognise him again?'

'Absolutely.' Duchene was keen to emphasise his value, given the somewhat complicated way in which the last days of the German occupation had unfolded.

'Very good,' Bennett said. 'That's one part of the problem solved. You're the only person we've found who's met him – or at least admitted to doing so. A lot of the German POWs clam up about who and what they knew. Not a surprise, but still frustrating.'

There was a pause as a gloved orderly, in black trousers and a white jacket, arrived with a tray holding iced tea in long glasses.

'What was your relationship with this Oberführer?' Brigadier Wright was the youngest of the trio, lean with a pencil moustache. It was the first time he'd spoken but his eyes hadn't strayed far from Duchene since he'd entered.

'Prisoner.'

'I understand you were arrested by him more than once? How did that happen?'

'You have very specific information,' said Duchene. 'Shame it's not so specific concerning your missing Oberführer.'

'It is. But that's not an answer.'

Leterrier seemed to bristle at this and leant forward in his chair, then reconsidered.

Duchene continued. 'They released me on the understanding that I would pass them information about a German major who was threatening me. I never intended to help them, so they arrested me again. You must have this already written down somewhere. Major Greer and Captain Martin said as much back in Paris.'

Greer shrugged.

Duchene nodded towards the closed folder on the coffee table. 'Is this a briefing or an interrogation?'

'A briefing,' said Bennett. 'This Oberführer is wanted for war crimes and with each passing week we're afraid the trail will grow cold. We've received reports that he was in Gestapo headquarters in Berlin as late as the middle of May. The Soviets have had the east locked down since April. We didn't pick him up as we came across the Elbe, and we've held the west of the city since June fifth.'

'Maybe the Russians arrested him. Or shot him.'

Wright brushed an already immaculate lapel. 'We don't believe so. We have intelligence that suggests they're hunting him as well.'

'A reliable source?' Duchene asked.

Leterrier glanced at Wright – a signal or a warning?

The brigadier held up his hand up, which could have easily been construed as being directed at Duchene as much as Leterrier. 'The source is classified, but it is someone from within their camp, yes.'

'We want the Oberführer before the Russians find him,' Greer said.

'And you have a plan for how this might take place?' Duchene asked.

'Obviously, that's where you come in. We'd like you to review some photos. Captured Gestapo. See if you can identify anyone from your meetings with the Oberführer. We're hoping that will get you started. Then you'll need to help our lead investigator to find and identify him.'

'That's you?'

'Ah no,' said Greer. 'Not my strong point. One of my men who's experienced with assignments such as this. We'll get you introduced as soon as we're done here.'

'I believe that's it.' Bennett said. 'Brigadier? Colonel?'

Both Wright and Leterrier shook their heads.

'Well, Mr Duchene, glad to have you on board. Good hunting.'

---

A breeze tugged at the dry grass that had overrun the drill field behind the barracks headquarters. Under the supervision of two soldiers, some local women were stacking rubble from what might have been a mess hall. The task seemed meaningless as the building had been levelled to all but its cornerstones.

Impervious to the heat, Greer strode across the grass, several steps ahead of Duchene, acknowledging a group of GIs jogging in full kit. Guards stood outside a barracks that was missing most of one wing, leaving it open to the elements. Greer, however, made his way to the front entrance, where he was saluted by the sentries, before holding the door for a puffing Duchene.

The smell of burnt wood lingered inside, a few blackened walls betraying its origins. Soldiers were lounging in various states of dress, reading, smoking and in one case listening to the radio. At Greer's arrival, the men leapt to their feet, but before they could snap to attention, Greer said, 'At ease, gentlemen. Take a goddamn load off. You've all earned it.'

The men laughed and relaxed.

An old ammunition trunk had been pulled into the centre of the room and two men had returned to sitting opposite one another on jerry cans, a small group of onlookers gathered around them. Greer made a beeline for the makeshift table.

'Captain Raye.'

He was addressing a dark-haired, broad-shouldered man, who was facing a wiry young corporal. Duchene assumed they were playing poker, so popular with the GIs he'd seen in Paris, but as he drew nearer he saw that the cards were laid out face up. Four were set out like the points of an unfinished star and the broad-shouldered man put down a final card to complete the pattern.

'This is the possible outcome if you follow the advice here and here, your past and the causes of your current situation.' He indicated two of the cards. There was something about his accent that Duchene couldn't quite place, something different to the other Americans he'd met.

'The card that's been revealed to you is death.'

The card was a worn ace of spades. Someone had used a pencil to draw in a skull, with the spade forming the nasal cavity.

'I don't understand,' the corporal said. 'She's going to die?'

'Oh, no... Death sounds bad, but it's not about someone dying. It would usually mean the death of something you'd planned, or, yes, a relationship with someone – you know, a split with your girl. But because this card is inverted it means it's not time for an end. It's saying, to me, that you need to be patient and hold true. Okay?'

The men around the soldier slapped the corporal on the back as the card reader stood.

He was about six foot, with a day or two of stubble on his face. That, and his uncropped curly hair, distinguished him from the others, all recently barbered. He wore only a sleeveless undershirt and on his right shoulder was a tattoo. Below a crudely drawn rosary were the words 'In memory of fallen brothers Ardennes 26.12.1945'.

He held out a hand. 'Sergeant Duchene. You're not in uniform?'

Greer sighed. 'He's still a civilian. Auguste Duchene, meet Captain Lewis Raye.'

Raye rubbed his chin. 'Hey, well, probably for the best. You'll have me if we need to throw our weight around.'

Greer pointed to the cards. 'You're still doing this?'

'They keep asking, sir, so I can't rightly refuse. Let me get my stuff.'

Raye pulled the cards into a stack and slipped them back into a battered box. He pulled on his shirt, but didn't button it, and grabbed a duffle bag from under his cot.

As they headed out of the barracks, he asked Duchene, 'You're okay to start now?'

'I am.'

'And they've fed you?'

'Just iced tea.'

'Major, any chance we can get something sorted out while we work?' Raye asked as they made their way through the heat towards the administration building.

Greer nodded. 'I'll ask a steward to bring something up to you.'

Then the major stopped and turned to Duchene. 'You don't want to be ordered to kill. Fine, so you're not military. But I'm giving you some advice here. Captain Raye might not be your commanding officer, but he knows what he's doing. Listen to him, stay close to him, and you'll get through this thing. He's gotten his men through much worse.'

# NINE

Duchene didn't mind the noise. In fact, he quite liked being surrounded by so much activity while sitting calmly in the middle of a bank of desks where studious clerks and intelligence officers reviewed reports, maps and aerial photography. Presumably nothing too classified. When he'd first entered, a few wary eyes had glanced up from pages, but only briefly before refocusing on Raye as he dragged a bouncing chair across the wooden floor to Duchene's desk. Raye hadn't appeared to notice this, or if he had, it didn't seem to bother him.

Now they sat eating sandwiches with the contents of a file box spread out before them.

'Okay, from what we can tell, these are all the Gestapo we picked up,' Raye said as he chewed.

'From what you can tell?'

'There are likely to be some that we've picked up but haven't identified yet, or won't. Things got hairy for the Germans there, at the end, and they were redirecting their resources to the front line – not much call for secret police when your capital is being obliterated. So we might have picked some up in SS uniforms or trying to pass as civilians, but not realised they were Gestapo. You can bet the Russkies also got some of them.'

'You think we won't find this Oberführer?'

'We might not. But I'd rather remain optimistic and be wrong. Not quite à vaillant coeur rien d'impossible, but something like it.'

'You speak French?' asked Duchene.

'French Creole. Not quite the mother tongue, but a version of it.' Raye smiled.

The accent finally fell into place.

'New Orleans born and bred. I'm actually Louis Rayé, but "Lewis Raye" was the best the recruiting officer could manage when I enlisted. Probably one of the reasons they put us together.'

'What are the other ones?'

'Not sure,' he said, clapping Duchene on the back. 'But I'm sure we'll find out soon enough.'

Duchene took another bite – canned meat and processed cheese. At any other time, an offence, but after months of rationing and going hungry, it was like a banquet.

Raye held up another photograph and Duchene leant in to look into the face. The man had a swollen eye and a broken nose – both bruised black, both fresh.

'Maybe,' he said.

Raye nodded and dropped it on the possible, as-yet-unrevealed pile. There was a second, larger stack for definite no's.

Raye held up another photo. 'We had a bet going if you'd even show.'

'We?'

'Corporal Austin and me.'

Duchene frowned. 'Who's Austin?'

'Mike. The driver. Brought you and the major from Tempelhof? Happy to say you won me five bucks.'

Another photo – a young face, haunted eyes, broken jaw.

'It would help me identify them if you took the photos before you started beating them.'

Raye glanced again at the image.

'This guy? Came to us like this. They're not always too keen on being captured.'

'But you had to check?'

'Well... sometimes they don't want to admit what they've been up to.'

'Up to?'

'War crimes, mass executions, death camps. These are not good people.'

Duchene shook his head at another photo. 'Is this what happens if you find the Oberführer?'

'Probably not. Higher ranks are processed differently. Unless you'd like some time with him by yourself, before we turn him over?'

'That's not who I am.'

'Fair enough. I just wasn't sure, since he'd arrested you. I thought maybe his guys had roughed you up.'

Raye took another bite out of his sandwich and followed it with a gulp of coffee. Hard scabs crested the ridges of his right knuckles. His forearms and face were pitted with older scars and cuts.

'How is it that you know so much about me?' Duchene asked.

'We have our intelligence.'

'From who?'

'I'd tell you, but I'm afraid that one is all wrapped up with the French. And I don't want to be betraying their trust in me. I do know they spoke with your daughter, when she was discharged. Seems she was concerned for you and wanted to go on the record about your work with the Resistance. Made it clear the Gestapo had arrested you a couple of times. I think that's what got them thinking you were a good fit.'

'Because if I was arrested I might have met the Oberführer?'

'Exactly. Leterrier is all caught up on why they put you back out onto the street, suggests you had some value to them.'

'Greer didn't say anything about that.'

'No, well, that's the major for you, he always holds something back. Me, I like to get it all out into the open. If we're going to be working together better, then we both know where we stand.'

'You're army intelligence as well.'

'Of course.'

Raye held up another photo. The whites of the man's eyes were visible beneath half-shuttered eyelids.

'He's dead.'

'No, passed out. Torture, executions, killings. Arresting Jews to send to death camps. You're a well-read man, you've heard of the Nuremberg Charter. Auguste, that's what we're doing here. We find this SS-Oberführer and bring him to justice. Yes, we interrogate him and, we hope, learn something that helps us find his commander, SS-Gruppenführer Heinrich Müller, so we can bring *him* to justice. You have to agree that sounds like a worthwhile cause.'

'Is that what we're doing here?'

'That's the plan.'

'Then, I agree. This is something worth doing.'

'Excellent.'

'Of course the Gestapo released me because they wanted me to gather evidence against a German officer. I didn't really have a choice. And since it was a German, I didn't think it was worth dying over my principles – if we're getting it all out in the open.'

'Appreciated. You do what you do to survive. I get it.'

Duchene took the next photo. The man had a thick neck, the flesh bunched below his boxer's ears. Dark eyes were set beneath heavy brows. A bent nose, long since broken and healed. Unlike the damaged subjects of the earlier photos, this man, whoever he was, smirked at the camera.

'I know him,' Duchene said. 'He was in Paris. He worked for the Oberführer.'

Raye burst out of his seat and moved to the open door, calling back to Duchene, 'What's the ID number on the back of the photo?'

'Three seven two.'

Raye shouted down the hall. 'Davis, grab me interview ID number three seven two.' Then he shoved the photos back into the box.

'Where are your bags?'

'With the driver.'

'Good. Drink your coffee, grab the sandwich.'

A young woman in uniform, her hair in a victory roll, arrived at the door with a document wallet.

'Good hunting,' she said, as Raye pulled his bag over his shoulder and rushed for the stairs. Duchene rushed behind him.

The interview report fluttered in the wind as the jeep raced down Altdorfer Strasse. Raye gripped the pages tightly while he scanned them. Duchene clung to a rear door handle as the vehicle swerved around a bomb crater. From the wheel, Mike Austin glanced at Duchene in the rear-view mirror. A grin was spreading beneath his sunglasses.

'I know what's in the basket,' he shouted over the sound of the rushing air.

Duchene said nothing.

Raye half turned, so that Duchene was seeing him in profile. 'His name is Udo Allmann. Ex-Geheime Staatspolizei and SS. Said he was stationed in Berlin. Nothing about spending time in Paris. Was very forthcoming – didn't have to be pushed to talk. When one of our tank divisions picked him up he was trying to cross the Elbe, driving a Kübelwagen with two box files of documents on the passenger seat. He'd taken them from the Gestapo headquarters and tried to use them to negotiate his surrender.'

'So where is he now? Is that where we're going?'

'Yes. I had all the Berlin Gestapo we'd identified pulled from the Rheinwiesenlager, the Rhine meadow camps, two days ago. We moved them to an old Nazi POW camp just down the road.'

'Just in case I came to Berlin?' Duchene shouted back.

'What did I say? I bet on your being here.'

'How many Gestapo did you move?'

'A few.'

They crossed a canal and continued south. On one side of the road the entire block had been reduced to broken bricks and stone. However, thanks to some random precision, the block behind it was still intact. The windows were no more, but the walls stood. Duchene could see glimpses of movement – a woman reading to two children seated on her knee, a man balanced on crutches, shaking out a blanket, three men reverently passing a cigarette between them.

On the other side of the road a row of young linden trees had been stripped of their lower branches, some cut with a saw, others hacked with an axe. Only their upper branches bore green heart-shaped leaves, fluttering in the summer breeze.

A long drive led up to the internment camp, which was surrounded by a double fence of barbed wire. These had recently been repaired, but the same attention hadn't been extended to what remained of the wooden watchtowers, several of which had fallen victim to shelling. Separated by more fencing was an administration building, beside which several American army trucks were parked.

Dozens of prisoners had been corralled in one area. They sat on the ground or the steps of two wooden bunkhouses patrolled by guards. Although large, the buildings were not capable of housing all the men.

'That's a lot more than a few,' Duchene said.

'What can I say? This is important,' Raye replied as he handed a folded piece of paper to a sentry who approached the idling jeep. 'OSS. We need to conduct an interview. Major General Bennett has approved.'

The sentry waved back to the watch-house. Three men strained against the sliding mechanism and rolled back the wood and wire gate. Austin put the jeep in gear and they entered the camp.

Duchene remained outside the administration building while Raye presented his papers. Austin, a cigarette between his lips, was poking a dandelion leaf into the basket.

Eventually, Raye re-emerged. 'They're getting him for us now.'

Duchene waited inside an empty bunkhouse. It had been long since abandoned. Many of the wooden shingles had fallen from the roof above, letting in shafts of late afternoon light. Long rows of bunks stretched ahead into the gloom and he could only just make out the back wall. A large mound of dark fabric filled one corner. In the gloom, it took him some time to realise that these were the discarded uniforms of the camp's original supervisors, the tell-tale black of the SS. There was a strong smell of animal musk in the room and at least three of the top bunks nearest to him were encrusted with bird droppings, which added a sulphurous note to the already mouldy air.

Raye was pacing the room, shoulders hunched, head thrust forward. He was like a coil of unspent energy ready to spring forward in a heartbeat.

A hinge complained as the door was pushed open and two guards brought in the man from the photo. He wore his dress boots and a frayed uniform, not dissimilar to the filthy pile in the corner. His jacket was off and his black SS shirt was bleached grey by the summer sun. His bull neck and broad shoulders were unchanged, but otherwise this was nothing like the muscled ape Duchene had encountered in Paris. He was thin, his clothes hanging from him. The only contradiction to his ill health was his skin, which had been burnt brown by long days in the sun.

'Udo Allmann?' Raye asked.

The man remained silent.

Raye gestured to a wooden seat and the guards pushed him onto it.

'Herr Allmann?' Raye repeated.

'SS-*Obersturmführer* Allmann,' Allmann replied, 'nicht *Herr*.'

'Actually,' Raye said in French, 'you'll find that you have no rank. You're designated a disarmed enemy. You're not even a prisoner of war. You're nothing – worse than nothing. You're Nazi scum.'

Raye's voice remained calm. Almost matter of fact. It wasn't clear to Duchene that Allmann understood him. He remained stone-faced except for the mention of the word 'Nazi', at which he smiled.

'I don't remember him speaking French,' Duchene said in English.

'Hard to be secret police if you don't speak the language, don't you think?'

Allmann was staring at Duchene. 'I know you,' he said in German.

'In Paris,' Duchene replied in the same language. 'August last year. You took me to meet the SS-Oberführer.'

Allmann nodded. 'You were helping us. To catch a political opponent.'

'Not helping,' Duchene replied, glancing at Raye. 'The Oberführer threatened me.'

Allmann laughed. 'Those were not threats. You would know if he had threatened you. You would still wear the marks on your body.'

'You were caught fleeing Berlin from Gestapo headquarters,' Duchene said. 'Is this the last place you saw the Oberführer?'

Duchene glanced at Raye, who seemed to pick up what he was saying and signalled his approval to continue.

Allmann shrugged. 'I may have. It was hard to know who was still there. A lot of Russians were trying to kill us, you know, so we were busy.'

'Busy stealing documents?'

'Collecting information. Information to trade. I could read the signs.'

'I don't doubt that. Russian shells and Allied bombs hitting your head. You'd have to be pretty stupid not to read those.'

'As you say, I am no fool.'

'Fool, no. But traitor, yes.'

'Ha. Not a traitor. Just outmanoeuvring. You French are weak, the Americans indulged. You have no idea what you're doing. You gather us up in fields, hundreds of thousands of men, ready to fight back when the werewolf howls.'

'I didn't see anyone out there getting ready to fight. Only tired men broken by war.'

'They will rise up when called.'

'With what? Sticks and stones,' Raye said in German. 'Because that's pretty much all you have. Your city has been bombed to shit. The war is over.'

Duchene stared at Raye as he continued.

'We're looking for the Oberführer. What is his name?'

'*Was.* He's probably dead now.'

Raye stepped calmly forward. 'Fine. What *was* his name?' He turned to Duchene and continued in German. 'Keen on the semantics, our friend. Wanting to make sure the mother tongue is respected.' Raye faced Allmann again. 'What was the Oberführer's name?'

'Fuck you...'

Raye placed his mouth next to Allmann's ear.

'What is his name?'

It occurred to Duchene that when this Gestapo had been healthy, back in Paris, he would have been twice Raye's size. Now he was just bone and loose flesh in a uniform, a uniform that was decaying like the dead body of the regime it stood for. This wasn't lost on Duchene, but it did seem to be lost on the German, who grabbed Raye by the neck.

A guard reached up to strike Allmann with his rifle, but he was too slow. Raye had already slammed his palm up into the German's chin, forcing him back with the chair, to crash onto the floor. Allmann, spitting blood, tried to get up as Raye stood with a foot on his chest.

'Go fuck yourself,' Allmann gurgled.

'We don't have time to do this the slow way,' Raye said to the guards. 'Take his arms.'

'You're going to torture him?' Duchene asked. 'He's a prisoner of war.'

'How many people do you think he's tortured and killed? He's too minor to get charged with war crimes, he's just going to go back into the pond and get shipped off somewhere to work off his debt to humanity. A beating is getting off easy.'

The two soldiers pulled Allmann to his feet, but before he was standing, Raye drove a fist into his face, knocking him back to the floor.

'Gentlemen, if you could?'

As they reached down again to haul him up, Duchene walked outside. It was after seven now, and the sun was journeying towards the horizon as the first stars began to appear in the sky. In the still evening the smack of fists on flesh carried across the compound. He lit a cigarette in the vain hope that it might distract him, but it did little to help. Distance was what he needed. He increased his pace.

Austin was sitting in the jeep, with the tortoise on his lap.

Duchene reached out a hand. 'Auguste,' he said.

'Michael. Mike.' The young man was holding another dandelion. 'He doesn't like the stems.'

'No,' Duchene said, scratching the animal's head. 'He's a fussy eater. Just flowers and leaves.'

'Does he have a name?'

'Ernest.'

'Like the writer?'

'Exactly. He's named after him. So you read?'

'Only properly since I came over here.'

Austin reached over to the passenger seat, opened the glove compartment and took out what looked like a stapled pamphlet, which he passed to Duchene. The cover showed a photograph of a bound copy of Edgar Allan Poe's *Selected Stories*.

'What's this?'

'The books the army sends us. That's how I heard about Hemingway. I've been looking for someone who has a copy of something by him. I'd trade both Davy Crockett and Marco Polo for that.'

'You've read this one?'

'A few times now.'

Duchene flicked it open and read the list of contents. Each long page contained two pages of a book printed side by side. 'Which is your favourite?'

'"Murders in the Rue Morgue" was good, but I also liked the "Masque of the Red Death". They lock themselves away from a plague, and have a party, but it still gets to them in the end. It's in the shape of a man, though, the plague.'

Duchene offered Austin a cigarette. 'I've read it. In French. Poe was popular in France before he found success in America.'

Duchene could see Raye wrapping his fist in a cloth as he emerged from the bunkhouse and headed towards them.

'Can you tell me something?' he asked Austin.

'Sure.'

'When we were back in there, the Gestapo, Allmann, said something about a werewolf's call.'

Austin nodded. 'Yes, the Werwolf – we've heard about them. It's all the Germans could talk about when we got here. And the few Russians I've spoken to. In the last days there were all these radio broadcasts calling on the werewolves to rise up. It's a codename, I think, for Nazi resistance.'

'And have they? Resisted?'

Austin shook his head. 'Nothing. We were told to keep an eye out for them, but nothing.'

'Thanks.' Duchene handed the book back. 'I like "The Cask of Amontillado". Revenge makes for good stories.'

'What's this about revenge?' Raye said as he lit a cigarette.

'There's a lot of it in Poe,' Duchene said, indicating the book.

'Ah, yes.' Raye patted Austin's shoulder. 'He likes reading. A good thing too, with all the sitting around and waiting he has to do.'

There was something changed about Raye. He had seen a man of pent-up energy, a soldier ready for action, for purpose. But now, as he stood here, cupping his swollen right fist, Duchene saw something else: release. That energy gone, directed into the face and body of a starving war criminal. Duchene knew he didn't have a moral compass for this sort of landscape, he doubted anyone did, but he did mark the moment. There was more to Raye than he'd considered.

'So I have a name.' Raye looked towards the setting sun and drew again on the cigarette. 'And the name of his daughter.'

***

'SS-Oberführer Volker Sprenger.' Raye was speaking into a black telephone handset attached to a signalman's radio backpack while scrawling his signature on pages held out by an army clerk.

Duchene stood beside him, watching the dusk spread across the shattered city.

'Yes sir, I'm releasing them all – just signing for that now. They can be taken back to the meadow camps. We also have a name for his next of kin, his daughter, Birgitta. She married Johann Kruger. We should check the internment records, in case we already have him.'

'You won't,' Duchene said. 'He's vigilant. Clever. He never gave me his name during the occupation. He was concealing his tracks even then. We need to start at the beginning with the daughter, of course.'

'If she's alive,' said Raye.

'That's always going to be the question in a place like this. Sprenger could be dead as well.'

'Alright.' Raye spoke into the phone again. 'We need some of the girls to get back into the office. Start working through the phone books and get us some coordinates for possible locations. Last known address of Birgitta and Johann Kruger.'

Raye paused, listening with his hand over the receiver. 'General wants to make sure you appreciate the complexity of finding a building, let alone a person.' Raye removed his hand. 'Yes, sir, I think he knows that – he's seen the city. Thank you, General.'

He replaced the receiver and thanked the signalman who'd been monitoring the call on a headset, slapping him on the back and offering him his Lucky Strikes.

'Excuse me, sir,' the signalman said, taking a cigarette, 'but are you Captain Raye?'

'I am.'

'The boys were talking and they said you come from voodoo country, have a gift for card reading?'

Raye inclined his head. 'That's what they say. You got something you need to know?'

'I haven't heard from my mother in a while. She wasn't well in the last letter she sent me. Just wanting to know, that's all.'

Ray pulled the battered deck of cards out of his pocket. 'Let's set up on the jeep.'

With his jacket spread on the bonnet as a surface for the cards, it took Raye ten minutes to complete the reading. The young man's mother had taken a turn for the worse but was on the mend. Any letters he could send would give her comfort.

'Back to camp, sir?' Austin asked.

'No, we'll start at daybreak. Let's get Mr Duchene quartered and then go from there.'

'Quartered?'

'We have a hotel in Kreuzberg, closer to the action. State department, officials, sometimes officers stay there. As you've seen, Andrews doesn't have much by way of accommodation.'

Only some of the streetlights on the roads that led them north towards the Spree were still working, so Austin relied on his headlamps to keep them free from trouble. Often, he would have to slow to a crawl to manoeuvre through the rubble. Beyond the streets the city was almost completely dark. Only the occasional tallow lamp or small fire lit the sockets of the apartment buildings or hinted at the dark outcrops of ruins in the blackness.

Several times Austin had to stop and check his compass and map before adjusting their route. In these moments Raye watched their surroundings, his hand on his sidearm.

When they were moving again, Duchene spoke. 'Are there partisans in Berlin?'

'Maybe.'

'They're called Werwolf?'

'Apparently. There was a lot of talk about them from the Germans while we were coming in. But the closer we got to Berlin, there were no insurgents, or secret SS snipers or anything like that. We only saw old men, veterans from the First World War, and boys in scraps of uniform – Hitler Youth. Pointless deaths without meaning.'

'Like all wars.'

'I disagree, but I can see why you would think so. You fought to bring the Germans into line. Twenty years later they were at it again, but it was worse because this time they invaded most of Europe. I get it.' Raye tapped his left shoulder. 'But my guys, they died for a reason. Because we were stopping the Germans, once and for all.'

'I hope you're right about that.'

'Anyway, it's not the Germans you should be worried about now. You'll want to keep a close eye on our Russian allies.'

There were more lights on the streets now, less rubble strewn on the road, even some signs. Austin was able to increase his speed, though watching for people, who were more numerous nearer the city centre.

The Grand Hostel Berlin, its windows shining with light, stood on a block that had suffered minimal damage from the bombings. Its decorative white façade had been cleaned of brick dust, and only a few bullets had pitted its walls. There was even a bellhop who came rushing past the armed American guards in the lobby and down the entrance steps when the jeep pulled up. Duchene had seen grander hotels in Paris, but took heart at the sight of an unscathed building that spoke of Berlin's past.

Raye leapt over the jeep's closed door and helped Duchene with his luggage. 'Keep an eye on that one,' he said, as he picked up his valise. 'Nothing a Berliner wants more than a way to carry their belongings around when their apartments collapse.'

'Are you serious?'

'They might have surrendered but they're still opportunistic. Suitcases and bicycles – they can't get enough of them.'

'I mean are you serious about the apartments collapsing?'

'Yes. Unstable walls – they're still falling down. Here.' Raye handed Duchene an envelope. 'Show this at the front desk. They'll take care of you.'

'You're not coming in?'

'No, not yet. Austin and I have to see a man about a horse.'

Austin started the engine as Raye got back into the jeep. 'Meet you in reception at zero six thirty.' Duchene watched them drive into the night before handing his suitcase to the bellhop.

**Friday, 3 August 1945**

# TEN

Duchene decided on breakfast in the bar. After struggling through another restless night of bad dreams about Marienne, he wanted some normality, and eating in public without the threat of vigilante justice felt as though it might be the solution. The hotel was busy with American visitors, men mostly, whose morning attention was drawn to reports and briefs.

His omelette was well made and the coffee was strong. A waiter even appeared to light his cigarette. He felt as though some life was returning to him. Even more remarkably, when he asked for an aspirin, one appeared soon after with a glass of water. Sitting here in his linen suit he could almost pretend that the world was whole again.

It took only a second for the illusion to dissolve once he stepped outside. The hotel faced a canal across which Duchene could see what was left of Berlin's central district. Entire blocks had been levelled to dust while collapsing apartment complexes stood like solitary observers to the devastation. The steel frames of domes and spires marked out those larger, more robust buildings that had been used as defensive points. But even these had been so battered by heavy fire that their once-sharp edges had little definition against the rubble behind them.

Duchene blinked in the bright morning light as a repainted German motorcycle with a sidecar pulled up. The driver, wearing grey trousers and a white shirt, called up to Duchene.

'Hop in.'

It was Raye.

Duchene stubbed out his cigarette. 'Mind the radio.'

On the floor of the sidecar was a signalman's radio pack. Clipped to its side, a medic's kit.

'We're going to the Russian quarter.'

Ray grinned. 'You're no fun. Always with the answers before I can surprise you. Birgitta Kruger's last known address was 22 Planckstrasse in Mitte. And Mitte is in the Soviet zone.'

⁕

The motorcycle cut through the streets, weaving between craters and rubble and around the remains of a tram car. It didn't take long before they reached a boulevard that had been completely cleared of debris, and Raye slowed. A few temporary guardhouses had been placed at intersections along both sides of the street. Those on the southern side were occupied by US soldiers, those to the north by their Soviet counterparts – young men, staring at one another, unsure if they were the new enemy.

'We're going around,' Raye said and followed a street that ran parallel to the crossing points. At the side of the Spree, he took the bike down a series of broken steps, Duchene juddering along with the radio as they descended onto the paved bank of the river.

Raye turned the throttle and they sped along beside the water past submerged houseboats and barges.

They'd followed the bank for only a few minutes before Raye found another set of steps that had been ripped up at their centre. The bike's front tyre slipped and started to churn earth. Raye pushed with his legs and gave the throttle another turn. The back wheel caught and the bike started moving again. In moments, they were back at street level.

'The Soviets don't patrol the crossing points?'

'They do, just not well. Too many rat lines – unguarded backways – so it's not too difficult for us to make an unofficial visit. I imagine it's the same for them. I'm sure their people cross to our side. How are you with a map?'

'A map in this?' Duchene gestured around him.

'You'll just have to give it a shot. Here, if we can follow the Spree we should get close. I've marked the address, if it's still there.'

It took half an hour of wrong turns and blocked roads before they arrived at their destination, a street where rubble women were working, handing blocks down a chain to be placed along a still standing wall. As the bike cruised down the street, children looked up from drawing pictures on a large piece of broken slate. Had it still been standing, the address would have been a small apartment block. Only two walls remained, the rest of the building having crashed inwards, bringing with it at least three storeys. It could have been more, but the roof that might have helped to define the building's original height was no more.

'Shit.' Raye brought the bike to a halt.

'Hold on a moment.' Duchene hauled himself out of the

sidecar, then approached the remaining wall, which faced the street.

The sound of the bike had caught the attention of the locals. A few people emerged from a bunker on the opposite side of the street, their expressions disoriented, their eyes blinking at the light. At the opposite end of the street, three Red Army soldiers had also appeared.

Duchene felt the blood rush from his face.

'Work detail. Should have known it was supervised. You might want to be quick.' Raye had left the bike running.

'They'll want to arrest us?'

'More likely come over and try to steal the bike. We need to hurry.'

The heavy doors still attached to the entrance had been forced open by a flood of bricks and rubble, but Duchene could see that messages had been scratched with knives and nails into the wooden surface: *Gerta Hinkel has left. Gone to Sonderburger Strasse 298, Mitte. Anna Bauer now at Wackenbergstrasse 92, Pankow.*

He called to Raye. 'They're names of the residents and where they went to.'

The soldiers were walking towards them. Their rifles were still slung but they were picking up speed.

'Is she there?'

Duchene scanned the scrawl. The door had been split by bullets, some rounds still lodged where they hadn't punched through. In other places, shrapnel had gouged and torn into the names and the details of the destinations.

'Auguste...'

*Birgitta Kruger moved to Lüderitzstrasse 5, Wedding.*

'Got it,' Duchene shouted. He raced to the sidecar, stumbling over the rubble, as the Soviet soldiers began to run, pulling their guns off their shoulders.

'Halt!' one shouted.

The women dropped their bricks and, crouching low to the ground, moved to either side of the street. As Raye tore down the road, it occurred to Duchene that none of the women had seemed startled or afraid.

'If she's still there, I'll buy you a drink,' Raye said as he sped back towards the steps at the river.

From the map, Duchene could see that, to reach Wedding in the French zone, they had gone the long way around the inner city. It would have normally been a short journey if you assumed free passage and working roads. But they had already risked travelling in the Soviet zone and as Raye explained, he didn't have rat lines everywhere. Instead they returned to Kreuzberg and followed the boroughs clockwise around the edge of the Soviet zone until they arrived at their destination.

As they worked their way through the wreckage, Raye presented his service card at the Allied checkpoints they encountered. Even though Duchene had now spent a full twenty-four hours in the city, the extent of the destruction continued to numb and overwhelm him. He tried to give it meaning in some way he could understand but found himself recalling the dystopian landscapes used by Renaissance painters used to portray the Last Judgement, and this did nothing to reassure him.

Duchene called for Raye to stop. Bricks had been stacked three rows deep around a U-Bahn entrance, which he could use as a landmark. He found it on the map and plotted a course.

'Turn left onto Seestrasse and then your next right will be the street we want.' Duchene braced himself as the bike accelerated and they took the turn.

They didn't have to look far to see their destination.

Four men were marching a pair of women out onto the street. One woman wore a cap with simple pants and a shirt. The other was in an elaborate floral dress, her hair tied back with a scarf.

'Best clothes...' Duchene said. *So why one and not the other?*

'Stop,' Duchene said. His command wasn't required; Raye had noticed the same thing. He killed the engine.

The men were walking both women away from an apartment entrance. After a quick count, Duchene said, 'That would be number five – Birgitta Kruger.'

Duchene breathed deeply, letting his eyes move without intention, reacting to the moment. The woman in the dress was holding her head down, keeping her eyes to the ground. The woman in cap, her head up, was talking, watching the men – she was commanding them. The woman in the dress was being arrested.

'They're Soviets!' Duchene whispered.

'How can you be sure?'

'Those men – they're wearing army boots. Look. I think the woman in the cap is in charge.'

Raye kept still but spoke with urgency. 'There are two pistols under your seat. Take one and give me the other.'

Duchene obeyed. 'You could hit Birgitta,' he said.

'And they could shoot us dead,' Raye said, pulling back on the slide.

'They might be unarmed.'

'That's some wishful thinking. They're all wearing jackets. Who does that in this heat?'

As if to underline the point, the Soviet woman removed her cap to wipe her brow. Dark hair tumbled free. It was Sabine.

# ELEVEN

'Who's Sabine?'

Raye leant towards Duchene from the back of the motorcycle. The summer heat was pushing sweat from his brow and a large drop hit the top of the sidecar.

'My wife,' Duchene gasped.

'Your missing wife? The communist?'

'Yes.'

Raye sucked air between his teeth.

Below the puffed sleeves of her blue summer dress, Birgitta's pale skin was sunburnt, the red more lurid than the dark auburn of her hair, which was held back by the scarf. Although her eyes remained locked on the cobblestones beneath her feet, she moved with confidence as she crossed the road. Sabine now held her firmly by the arm.

'Fuck.' Raye scanned the men. 'Can you ride a bike?'

'What? No.'

'It's easy. Right-hand is your throttle. Go slow. That's speed. In front of that, the brake. But don't stop unless I tell you.'

Raye stood up, then quickly slid into the sidecar.

'Take us in close. I'll do the rest.'

'You can't shoot them.'

'I will if they draw on us.'

'Not Sabine.'

'Listen, my plan is to get us out of there fast. So no one has time for a gun fight.'

'How did they find Birgitta?'

'They might have known the Oberführer's name. We need to move fast. They'll notice us but play it cool. Pull your hat down and keep the bike moving slowly. Nothing too strange, just two people riding down the street.'

Duchene sat on the bike, turned the key in the ignition. The sound drew the attention of the Soviets. He applied the throttle too hard, bringing the bike forward with a hop.

'Easy,' Raye whispered.

He rolled the throttle more gently this time and they moved gradually towards the group.

*Sabine.* His mind was struggling to form the connections. She'd retreated from Spain with what was left of one of the International Brigades, after the fascists had defeated them at Ebro.

One of the Soviets started to reach under his jacket.

'Now!' Raye shouted and Duchene accelerated.

Raye fired over the heads of the Soviets, who hit the ground, moving low to take cover along the walls. Two now held pistols.

'Get close to her,' Raye said, firing again.

It had the intended effect. Birgitta crouched immediately; Sabine reached down to pull her back up. Duchene's heart was pounding – they were coming in too fast. His hat flew off and Sabine looked him dead in the eyes.

Confusion spread across her face, which showed lines that were not part of his memory of her. Her skin was tanned but for a pink scar running along one cheek. Her eyes were alert as ever, taking in Duchene, the bike and Raye beside him, pulling the German woman into the sidecar.

The two Soviets by the wall raised their guns.

'Ne strelyay!' Sabine shouted, holding up her hands to stop them. The men hesitated as she barked more commands in Russian.

Birgitta was screaming in protest as Raye struggled to get her into the sidecar.

'We're saving you,' he shouted. 'From the Red Army.'

Birgitta's green eyes locked with the American's. Hard as steel.

The bike roared on. Wind was rushing over them, pulling at their clothes and stripping sweat from exposed skin.

'I'm going to stop,' Duchene yelled. He was beginning to run out of road. The intersection ahead was blocked with rubble.

'Right foot, push down – that'll slow your back wheel. Then bring in the front.'

Duchene pushed down with his foot, too hard, before snapping the front brake tight with his hand. The bike skidded, turned sideways and came to a stop. Raye and Birgitta clambered out of the sidecar.

'We need to keep moving on foot while I call for some help.' Raye pulled the radio onto his back and grabbed the second pistol from under the seat, then turned to Birgitta.

'I'm American. He's French. We're trying to get you away from them. Do you understand?'

'Yes,' she replied.

'Good.'

Ray pulled the keys from the bike and stuffed them into his pocket. 'Let's lose them and then we can make the call.'

# Paris
## Saturday, 14 November 1936

# TWELVE

A haze of cigarette smoke beneath the ceiling conspired with the low wattage of the hanging bulbs to make the light in the restaurant even more gloomy. People sat in small groups at tables in dark corners and spoke in urgent whispers over plates of oily cassoulet and cups of coffee.

'Table for two,' Duchene said to the approaching waiter, who nodded and led them over to a round table that wobbled as soon as Duchene placed his elbow on it. The menu on the wall was brief and dusty.

'A bottle,' Sabine said. 'The burgundy.'

'There's a lot that's not right about Vincent's death.' Duchene whispered in deference to the prevailing mood.

'His being murdered for a start.'

'The reason, more importantly.'

'Why are we here?' Sabine asked.

'The man I spoke to last night, as we were leaving –'

'Claude, yes?'

'He came up to me, offered to help in any way I needed.'

'He was a friend of Vincent.'

'I asked him if anyone knew where Vincent was going when

he left party headquarters. He took me to another man, who found someone else, a woman named Annabelle. It took a few conversations, but I eventually found someone who told me that this place, Le Drapeau, was where Vincent had planned to have a meal. He often did.'

'You've been busy.'

You too, Duchene thought, recalling Sabine's lengthy conversation with Bloyer after the meeting of the party leadership.

'So what happens next?'

The waiter returned with their wine. His waistcoat was fraying around the edges and a button was missing.

'Anything to eat, Monsieur, Mam'selle?'

That often happened, the Mam'selle. Their age difference often led to assumptions about their relationship that many men would have appreciated. Initially, Duchene had too, enjoying the idea that he was sufficiently attractive to have a mistress. Now it was a reminder of their difference not just in years, but also in aspirations.

Sabine lifted the silver chain around her neck to reveal her wedding band. Factory work made it difficult to preserve rings worn on hands.

'*Madame*, thank you,' Sabine said. 'This is my husband.' The waiter shrugged. 'We're still deciding.'

She returned her gaze to Duchene. 'So that's what you meant by going back to the beginning?'

Sabine's gaze was intense, her brow slightly furrowed. Without prompting, like him she had dressed for the street. Where he wore a coat and grey suit, she was in a practical skirt and a jacket, nothing to mark her out or otherwise draw attention. Duchene smiled at her, his intelligent wife. So much about this moment reminded him of why he adored her.

Duchene lit a cigarette and offered it to her. 'It is what I meant. That death threat wasn't specific enough to mark the beginning of what happened to Vincent. So we go to the next thing we know about the last time he was seen alive – his leaving the office and coming here.'

'And not start with where his body was found?'

'That would probably be better,' Duchene replied. 'It's how the police work. But because they're there, we're here.'

The waiter moved with exacting caution as he cleared a table, placing the plates carefully down his arm, pausing, so as not to interrupt, before taking away a greying napkin.

'What is this place?' he asked.

Sabine chuckled. 'Ah, a restaurant. We're not going to get very far if I have to explain to you everything that's obvious.'

'Very funny. Who comes here? Dissidents?'

'Yes, something like that, anarchists, militant socialists, a few Workers of Zion. I guess we can include card-carrying members of the PCF on that list, if Vincent ate here regularly.'

The discussions at the tables started to make sense now – separated by enough distance to ensure privacy but with a shared understanding. He knew there were the political cafés where Marxists, communists and socialists would openly debate their ideological differences and engage in verbal brawls to position themselves with their colleagues as champions of their cause. This, though, was not a place of theatre and posturing, but one of negotiation, deal-making and information exchange.

'Are we eating?' Sabine asked.

'You tell me. Do you think the party would assume that our stipend would be spent on meals?'

'I think this expense is acceptable,' she smiled. 'But make sure you check first.'

Duchene waved the waiter over and Sabine ordered civet de sanglier for each of them.

Marienne might be having lunch now too, or perhaps she was out somewhere with Camille, helping her with an errand, or just reading while their neighbour refined a piece on the piano. Marienne was old enough to spend time in their apartment, if she preferred, as long as Camille was next door and she accompanied her if she needed to go somewhere. Like her mother, Marienne was already germinating the desire to explore the world and take in its wonder. And like her mother she didn't appreciate that this pleasure would bring with it equal parts of pain. Duchene could only delay her roaming for so long by channelling her curiosity and passion towards books. Safe worlds on paper, worlds without risk. As her confidence grew, so too would her longing to make her own discoveries, pursue her autonomy and rebel against her parents. It was only a matter of time before the offer of having the apartment to herself was no longer a thrill and she would become secretive and elusive, away in Paris on errands of her own.

'May I have the photo?' Duchene asked.

Even in black and white it was easy to imagine Vincent's wine-fuelled complexion and its web of thin veins. With his balding head and close-set eyes, it was obvious that he hadn't possessed the physical appeal, elegance and charisma of someone like Bloyer. This was a man who had fought for the underdog, a street agitator and union boss, a man whose action and passion appealed to his supporters.

'Would the kitty extend to ten francs?'

'That's half of tomorrow's stipend.'

'It may be important.'

Sabine passed him a note, which he placed flat on the table, with the photo on top of it.

The waiter returned with the boar stew, positioning the plates carefully.

Duchene placed a hand on his sleeve. 'Excuse me a moment, I was wondering if you could help us with something?'

'More wine?'

'No thank you. A question about someone who you may have seen here – last Wednesday.'

The waiter glanced at the photo. There was a flash of recognition in his eyes before he tried to conceal it with indifference.

'We observe the privacy of our clientele. I'm sure you understand.'

Duchene turned the photo just enough to let the denomination of the note peek from behind it.

'It's nothing too personal. We'd just like to know if you saw him that evening. If he ate alone? If he mentioned anything about where he might be going? Perhaps something you might have overheard if he was with a companion.'

The waiter scanned the room, then took the note and tucked it into the pocket of his waistcoat.

'He was eating with someone. A Trotskyist.'

'How could you know that, unless it was Trotsky himself?'

'I overheard them. They were discussing Trotsky.'

'Arguing?'

'No. Discussing – calmly.'

'You wouldn't be able to describe this man?'

'He wore a red scarf and he had a grey beard, but his hair was dark. He also had horn-rimmed glasses, octagonal. His accent was Marseille.'

'You seem to remember him well,' Duchene said.

'I notice these things when the clients leave a big tip. I'm going to remember you.'

'The Trotskyist left you a big tip?'

'No. This man.' The waiter tapped the photo. 'Three francs.'

'Thank you,' Duchene said.

'Trotskyists?' said Sabine as soon as the waiter had left.

'A defection? Do you think he was capable?'

'No,' she replied. 'He was enamoured with Stalin.'

'But that's how you would make a defection, isn't it? Conceal your discontent?'

'He'd only just been elected to the Central Committee.'

'So perhaps he was leaking information? I'm not the expert here, but I did pick up that your lot and the Trotskyists don't get along.'

Sabine shrugged. 'Personally, I don't care for the politics. I don't care about the internal squabbling of the Russians. It has been decreed that we make all efforts to discredit them.'

'Discredit?'

'Not their words exactly, more like, "Comrades, you must reveal to the proletariat the inherent flaws of their thinking and how it undermines the workers' struggle." Something like that.' Sabine spoke with a Russian accent while rolling her large eyes, exaggerating the joke.

And Duchene almost forgot that there was trouble below the surface, currents of dissatisfaction, and his resistance to them. The surface was always so enticing.

# THIRTEEN

The rain had returned and Duchene needed his umbrella. Sabine had her arm through his, the simple contact reviving his belief in a shared future. As always, the Parisians around them moved confidently along the wet pavements, using experience, following instinct. They cut corners, flowed neatly into the lines descending into the Métro and paused under shop awnings until traffic lights changed.

Duchene placed a hand on his wife's shoulder. 'Let's keep this new information to ourselves for now.'

'That we have someone who saw Vincent before he died?'

'Just that he's a Trotskyist. I think it's alright to say we have a description.'

'Because there's something that isn't right about his murder.'

'Exactly.'

'Care to elaborate?' she asked.

'It's a feeling. How quickly he was found in the Seine. If the murder was calculated, you'd have weighted the body.'

'Unless the fascists wanted to make a point.'

'If it was fascists.'

'Surely they're the most likely suspects.'

'Which is why this feels wrong. They are too obvious.'

Placing a finger on her lips, Sabine smiled, then brought the same finger to rest on Duchene's mouth.

'Silenzio,' she said.

Duchene shook his umbrella and they walked into the PCF headquarters.

Among those working the press. Duchene recognised the same thin young man, who called, 'Comrade Duchene!' and rushed over to greet Sabine.

'Um, it's –'

'Thomas, Thomas Renaud. And Monsieur Duchene. You've returned. Any news?'

'We should really talk to the Central Committee first.'

'Of course. You've seen today's edition of *L'Humanité*?' Almost before Sabine could shake her head, he dived back to his pamphlet satchel, which hung from the side of the press.

He passed her the broadsheet, already folded to the relevant article. Under the headline, 'Justice Coming for a Fallen Comrade', Renaud had given the time and date of the murder, before continuing:

> *Those who perpetrated this vile crime are still at large. But justice is coming for them! While the police have shown little interest in pursuing this case, a notable private investigator has offered his support to the PCF, under the guidance of longstanding member and active anti-fascist, Comrade Sabine Duchene. Yes, my dear associates, the PCF is not willing to stand by and let a comrade's death go unanswered.*

'Who agreed to this?' Duchene asked. The world around him fell away and his eyes fixed on the writer standing beside him. He barely registered that his hands were shaking and that the rush of blood to his face had brought with it a ringing in his ears.

Thomas looked pale. 'The Central Committee,' he said. 'I thought you would like it.'

Duchene flung the paper to the floor. 'Was it Bloyer?'

'He was there.'

Duchene started up the stairs.

'Auguste, wait,' Sabine called after him. 'Wait.'

She caught him on the second landing. 'What's the matter?'

'This puts you at risk. What if it is the fascists? They now have your name – they know you're looking for them.'

'I thought you said it wasn't the fascists.'

'Whoever it is, they will learn your name. Bloyer has done this. He's put you in danger.'

'We can't take it back.'

'But they must agree that this must not happen again.'

'Alright. Yes. Let's speak to them, but let's do it calmly.'

'Because it might embarrass you if we don't?'

'No, because that's the best way to convince someone.'

Duchene's hands were still shaking. He gripped the balustrade with his left and placed his right in a pocket. 'Fine.'

She grinned. 'Admit it, the real reason you're upset is because they said I was supervising you.'

They found Bloyer in a new office, on the fourth floor, sleeves rolled up, reading over papers, an open bottle of beer beside him.

'Comrade, Monsieur, so glad to see you so soon. This is excellent timing. Let me get the others.'

He smiled as he stood and pulled on a jacket, either ignorant of or unconcerned by the scowl on Duchene's face. The jacket, though cut from a utilitarian cloth, was tailored and fitted neatly across Bloyer's strong frame.

'I want to talk about that article in *L'Humanité*,' Duchene said.

'Ah, yes, that. Come along.'

Duchene and Sabine followed Bloyer into another office, where Langlois looked up at them over his half-glasses. A bust of Lenin sat on the corner of an orderly desk.

'Comrade. Monsieur.'

'Before you say anything,' Duchene said, 'we need to talk about that article.'

'The one Comrade Renaud wrote,' Bloyer said.

'We felt it was necessary for the morale of the party. That something was being done. That there would be consequences.'

'And you authorised it?' Duchene looked from Langlois to Bloyer.

'We did,' Langlois said.

'It's put Sabine in danger,' said Duchene.

Langlois held up a finger. 'It's put Vincent's murderer on notice.'

Duchene could feel frustration growing. 'That's the same thing. Now they know we're coming for them.'

'If it's any consolation, there was debate, and the decision wasn't unanimous,' Bloyer said.

'You only met last night. The presses would have already been running. You couldn't have waited a day?'

'We don't answer to you, Monsieur.'

'And what about Sabine? As a member of your party?' Duchene

was raising his voice now. 'We can stop the investigation right now if that helps to make the point.'

'Comrades, Auguste...' Sabine tucked her hands into her pockets and leant against the desk. 'I'm sure there's an agreement we can reach. We've already had some success, so it's worth considering my husband's requests, and as we were saying before, Auguste, there's nothing we can do to change what's done.'

'Perfectly reasonable suggestion,' Bloyer said. 'What would you like us to do?'

'No more articles, without discussing it with us first,' she said.

'And nothing more about Sabine – in *L'Humanité*, in your flyers, out there on the street.'

'I think we can agree to that, on behalf of the Central Committee, yes?'

Bloyer was speaking to Langlois, who tossed a pencil onto his desk. 'Fine.'

'Wonderful.' Bloyer clapped his hands. 'Now let's move on to your report.'

'Vincent met a man for dinner, last Wednesday. We'll need to do more investigating before we can provide you with a name,' Duchene said

'That's fast work. You Duchenes make a good team. Where did they meet?' Bloyer asked.

'At one of Vincent's regular haunts, Le Drapeau,' Sabine said.

'In the Latin Quarter. I know it.'

'Was the man a party member?' Langlois asked.

'We don't know at this stage,' Duchene replied.

'But you must have some idea of some kind of affiliation? There are just under three million people in Paris. A description is not enough to go on,' Langlois said. 'I've also heard of Le Drapeau, it's where militants meet.'

'So far,' said Sabine, 'we have only rumours and second-hand information. We don't want to cause any unnecessary distress to his family.'

'We're not his family, Comrade Duchene. You can be direct with us,' Langlois said.

'If we can agree to keep it among ourselves, he may have been meeting with a Trotskyist.'

Duchene blinked. It had taken only a second and he was back below the surface. He stared at Sabine. She was either ignoring him or was too focused on Langlois to register his glare. Bloyer glanced at him.

'Trotskyist? That doesn't make sense,' Langlois said. 'Vincent was Bolshevik through and through. There wasn't a Menshevik bone in his body. We spoke about the findings of the Supreme Tribunal in the USSR and he was firmly in agreement with the outcome.'

'I agree, Comrade Langlois,' said Bloyer, 'that it doesn't match with the little I knew of him, but perhaps we've been deceived all along – if you consider what we learnt earlier today.'

Duchene drew his eyes away from Sabine. 'You've learnt something about him. Something that would undermine the party.'

'Exactly,' Bloyer said. 'We're missing funds – a lot of funds: five thousand three hundred and ninety francs.'

'That's a very specific amount.' Sabine spoke without emotion, but she had turned very pale.

'I'm afraid it is,' Bloyer said. 'The money you raised for the

International Brigades. We hadn't had a chance to bank your contribution. The envelope was still in the safe, but the money was gone.'

'And no one else had the combination?' Duchene asked.

Sabine's hands were now out of her pockets and she was standing away from the table, staring at the bust of Lenin.

'Just Vincent and our treasurer, who's been in Lyon on party business for the last week,' Langlois said.

'But as you're no doubt surmising, Monsieur Duchene, this discovery and the new information about your Trotskyist doesn't paint a reassuring picture,' Bloyer said.

'The article said he had a family. Would he have risked exposure, his livelihood?' Duchene asked.

'To his shame,' Bloyer replied, 'Vincent's wife had moved with her children back to her father's farm. In Aquitaine. We understand they weren't speaking. As you can imagine, we won't be reporting the theft to the police.'

'If Vincent had taken the money to his apartment, then whoever killed him probably has it.'

'In which case it's likely it's gone forever,' Bloyer said.

'But we would appreciate it if you could include the theft in your investigation, if that's possible,' said Langlois. 'We'd like that money back.'

---

A cold wind was winding its way up the Seine and snaking like an invisible tributary along the boulevards and streets. It pulled at Duchene's raincoat and at the scarf around Sabine's neck. She had said nothing since they left Rue La Fayette, even during the Métro ride to the eleventh arrondissement and, now, continued to stalk beside him in silence.

'I can see how frustrating this must be.' Duchene spoke gently. 'I can't imagine how many hours it took, how hard you worked, to raise those funds.'

She glared. 'I don't care about myself, or the work. It's the people who gave it to me. They put trust in me, when money is hard to come by, and they did it because it would be put towards something meaningful. How could Vincent just take it? How could he betray their trust like that?'

'That is something we might still discover. But Sabine, my love, we must be as one on this. I'm serious when I say you need to be careful. That newspaper article… You shouldn't have said anything about the Trotskyist.'

'Bloyer and Langlois aren't going to say anything. Besides, they were already making assumptions based on the name of the restaurant.'

'And their assumptions are just that. We didn't need to confirm what we'd been told. What if it gets out there, to the Trotskyists, that the PCF is searching for one of them? They're capable of assassination. The party's Russian leadership is rife with it.'

'Is that what's worrying you? You don't have to be doing this.'

'I'm here because you asked me. I'm here to keep you safe.'

Sabine stopped walking. Her eyes narrowed, not in anger, but with an increased earnestness. Again, he felt the distance between them, physically, as though she was speaking from afar even though she was just centimetres away. 'What makes you think you can do that? The world is about to catch fire. How can you keep me safe from that? How is that your responsibility?'

'As your husband –'

'You can't be everywhere. When I'm in Spain, how can you keep me safe when you are in France? You need to understand that I can take care of myself.'

A shiver moved through him. 'So that's it, then. You're leaving us?'

'I think I am. Just for a year.'

'We haven't really discussed this.'

'It's something I need to do.'

'What about Marienne?'

'It tears at my heart, but I tell myself, she's ten, a strong ten, and no longer a baby. I need you to tell me that she will be fine, that you will both be fine, for a year.'

'It might not be for a year. Wars don't run to the clock. You could die.'

'I won't.'

'Belief doesn't stop bullets.'

'I'll have the two of you to return to. That will keep me alive.'

'And what if I say no?'

'Because you're my husband? Auguste, I married you because you're not that sort of man. I chose you for a reason.'

'I don't want you to go.'

'I know. But I must do this. I can't sit and watch fascists destroy the world. I want Marienne to see that there are ideals worth fighting for. That you should never betray your own self.'

'We're meant to decide these things together.'

'Auguste. My love for you, for Marienne, hasn't changed. But I need to be loyal to myself as well.'

He hadn't realised he'd started moving again. Sabine was only a few steps behind him, but he felt as though there were metres between them and that the distance was growing

---

It was not clear to Duchene how long he walked the streets. Eventually, the darkening sky and the streetlights flicking into life drew him out of his internal world. He didn't want to return to the apartment; he didn't want to face Sabine. But then came the thought of Marienne, and how she would respond when she learnt of her mother's decision. He desperately needed to be there, beside her.

He'd covered a lot of ground, but he found his bearings and some deep instinct steered him back into Saint-Ambroise. Then it took him only ten minutes, at pace, to reach the foyer of their apartment. He took the stairs to the first floor two at a time, his heart pounding as he reached the front door.

Sabine sat stone-faced at the dining table, Marienne beside her, an arm wrapped around her mother's shoulders. As soon as she saw Duchene she rushed over to hug him.

'You didn't wait?' Duchene was trying to push emotion aside so he could properly read the signs in the room.

'I haven't said anything.' Sabine's voice was flat and tired.

'Papa,' Marienne said, 'men were just here.'

'Who?' Duchene's body was suddenly coursing with adrenaline.

'Police.' Sabine had been looking blankly across the room, but now she blinked, and brought herself back. She stood up and started pacing. 'Fuck them. Fuck!'

'What did they do?' It felt as though his heart was trying to beat itself free of his ribs.

'Spoke to me.'

A copy of *L'Humanité* lay on the floor. There were two new cigarette butts in the ashtray he'd emptied this morning.

'They're closing the case. They're saying it was death by misadventure. It's going to be reported tomorrow. They said we wouldn't be safe if they read any more about it in the paper.'

'Were you here when they came?' he asked Marienne. 'Did they threaten you?'

'I asked her to go to her room while we talked,' Sabine said.

'I heard it,' Marienne said, her voice faint.

Duchene gripped his daughter more tightly.

'What did they say, exactly?'

'Just to stay away. They didn't go into detail.'

'Did they give you their names?'

'Of course not.'

'Are you alright?'

'I'm fine. Angry.'

'How can misadventure have led to him being stabbed?'

Marienne looked up at Duchene, slowly letting go of his waist.

'I don't know,' Sabine said. 'Being a communist? It says he contributed to his own death. I guess they'll say he drowned.'

'But they think it's the fascists,' said Duchene.

'Yes. Clearly they're trying to minimise it.'

As though his body was leading him, Duchene held his hands towards her. 'We have to stop,' he said.

'Stop?'

'They've come into our house.'

'And what about the money?'

Duchene said again, 'They've come into our house.'

'I know. Listen, Bloyer and Langlois have agreed not to publish anything until they've spoken to us. We can still search for the Trotskyist, look for the money. Any threat is related to our contradicting the police finding – so we never contradict it. But it doesn't stop us from trying to solve it.'

Marienne was now curled on the couch, watching them, eyes wide, taking it all in.

Duchene took a deep breath. 'Fine. If that's what you want to do. But I'm putting another bolt on the door. And we all need to lock it whenever we're in. All of us.'

Sabine stopped pacing. 'Thank you.'

## Sunday, 15 November 1936

## FOURTEEN

'You understand I'm only talking to you because I want to make it clear that we had absolutely nothing to do with the death of Marcus Vincent.' The elderly man put his pipe back in his mouth. Smoke traced its way through a thick, well-groomed moustache and around the edge of his bowler hat before dispersing into the air.

Although Sabine may have forced Duchene's hand by revealing the Trotskyist connection, there were still back channels and lines of communication open between the moderates of the party and their counterparts within the Troskyist factions. This was how they had found their way, via Langlois, to Gérard Montfort.

Around them, the mossy roofs of tombs still dripped with the morning's rain. A few birds hopped between lichen-encrusted branches.

'Who chose the location?' Montfort asked, as smoke rose again from the pipe.

'The cemetery?' asked Sabine.

'No, Kardec's grave.'

'I did,' Duchene replied, tapping the tip of his next cigarette on a match box.

'Very droll, Monsieur, meeting at the grave of the father of spiritism in order to discuss the recently deceased.'

'Shame this Kardec isn't still alive,' said Sabine. 'We could just ask him who killed Vincent.'

'Ha. Well, yes. I did want to formally say that we were saddened by Comrade Vincent's demise. We may not have seen eye to eye, but his passion for the workers was well known.'

They wound their way up a path between the graves of Père-Lachaise, past two gardeners who had finished raking the last of the autumn leaves onto large hessian squares. Montfort placed a hand on one man's arm and spoke quietly to him. The gardener nodded and tipped his cap at the old Trotskyist.

Duchene turned to check on Marienne, who was walking behind them, out of earshot but not out of sight. She looked like a small mourner in her black coat. As an inducement to her joining them on their journey to the edge of the city, Duchene had agreed that they could visit some of the more elaborate tombs – those with statues or that looked like doorways into the underworld. There was a lot of walking still ahead of them.

'Thank you for your willingness to talk to us,' Sabine said. Her prominent role in supporting the International Brigades had made her an acceptable intermediary. 'We wish to ask specifically about a man who might have met Comrade Vincent.'

'From Marseille. Horn-rimmed octagonal glasses. Dyed his hair but not his beard,' said Duchene.

'You're describing Aaron Meunier.'

'You identified him very quickly,' Duchene said.

'That's because he's missing and we're concerned about his welfare. He was returning to Paris and we were expecting to have heard from him by now.'

'You've been to his apartment?'

'He doesn't have one – he usually stays a boarding house. I'm not encouraged by the connection with your Vincent. I hope there's a simple explanation, but I'm beginning to fear that something might have happened to him as well.' Montfort placed his hand on his chest. 'May we sit for a moment? I had forgotten how the ground slopes here.'

Sabine nodded towards a bench that sat along the edge of a corridor of ash trees, their branches meeting to form natural tunnel. Duchene waved to Marienne, who smiled back at him as she stopped to perch on the edge of a grave. After checking the stone for dampness, she took out *Murder in Mesopotamia* and resumed her reading.

'She's a patient one, your daughter.'

'We would have left her at home, but we had a surprise visit from the police last night,' Sabine said.

'Oh dear. I hope you weren't harmed?'

'Just threats,' Sabine replied. 'What makes you think Meunier's is in danger?'

'Other than meeting your colleague, who is now dead? I'm sure you've been keeping up with events in Moscow – the purging of our leadership, Trotsky's expulsion from Paris and now his arrest in Norway by Quisling's fascists... It's not a good time to be a Bolshevik-Leninist. I know, from his last correspondence, that Comrade Meunier was planning to buy a gun when he reached the city.'

Montfort puffed on his pipe as his left hand, again, rested briefly over his heart.

'Did he?' Sabine asked.

'No idea. When you told me that he'd met Vincent, it was the first I'd heard of his arrival in Paris.'

Duchene lit another cigarette. 'You're not going to let us look at his letter, are you?'

'I beg your pardon?'

'The letter. In your breast pocket. You keep moving your hand there.'

'I – what?'

'I'm assuming it's from Meunier. You have it with you now, not because you intended to show it to us, but because you want to keep it safe. It reveals something about what he was doing.'

'Oh ho, Monsieur, you're grasping at shadows.' Montfort's neck, already a shade of red, started to darken.

Sabine looked at Duchene, who nodded briefly.

'Comrade,' she said, 'one thing is clear from our meeting today: there is a connection between these two men. Which means we're after the same answer. I can promise you that we will tell you everything we discover about Comrade Meunier, but we need somewhere to turn next. Are you sure there's nothing more you can tell us that might help?'

Montfort stopped puffing and watched them both from the seat. He pointed the stem of the pipe towards Sabine.

'You may feel Stalin is in the ascendant now, and that we're in a defensive retreat, but times change, the world shifts. We're unlikely to remain in this position and I'm not one to forget a broken promise, Comrade Duchene.'

'I understand,' Sabine replied.

'Good.'

They waited as Montfort repacked his pipe with tobacco. 'He did say where he was staying – a rooming house.'

'So why haven't you been there already?' Duchene asked.

'Fear, Monsieur. Stalin sends the NKVD overseas to do his bidding.'

'NKVD?'

'The People's Commissariat of Internal Affairs,' Montfort said. 'His secret police. I'm not proud to say it but there it is – Comrade Meunier isn't the only Trotskyist who fears for his life.'

❦

The boarding house tilted over the narrow, cobbled alleyway, forced into a slow lean by the fifth and sixth storeys, which had been added in more recent years. The streaks on its grey walls betrayed their origins as more rain sent rivulets through the grime. Duchene and Sabine passed under a crude walkway that connected the fifth floor of the miserable building to a tenement balcony opposite. From this hung tattered ropes and animal sinews that had at one time been used to reinforce the crossing.

Broken bottles and rotting vegetables were strewn around the entrance, the only part of the boarding house that showed any sign of being maintained. Freshly cut wood had been used to reinforce a door that stood open.

The foyer had just enough space to fit both Duchene and Sabine, its narrowness exacerbated by a large woman who sat on a chair at the foot of the stairs. It was unclear if she was sneering or smiling; her teeth, like the peeling paper on the walls around her, were yellow and mottled.

'Price is eighteen francs a night,' she said.

'We're here to check on a friend,' Sabine said. 'We shouldn't be long.'

'Eighteen francs a night,' she repeated. 'That includes visitors.'

Sabine smiled and passed her the money, which she stuffed into a pristine velvet purse. Duchene noted, by the woman's chair, a club from which half a dozen nails protruded. He smiled and tipped his hat.

The woman spat onto the sawdust-covered floor. Duchene noted where the globule had marked its landing place. He was unsure whether she was clearing her throat or showing disdain. Perhaps both.

'What's the name?'

'Aaron Meunier, but he may not have used his real name,' Sabine said.

The woman lifted up a torn ledger that was resting against the chair. 'No Meunier. What other name did he use?'

'Not sure,' Sabine replied. 'He wears funny-shaped horn-rimmed glasses. Black hair and grey beard.'

'R. Fornier. Fourth floor, fourth room. Remind him the rent is due tomorrow.'

'How many nights did he pay for?' Duchene asked.

'Arrived last Monday. Paid for a week in advance.'

Duchene tipped his hat again and set off, Sabine right behind him.

A trickle of water was running down the handrail, its source somewhere in the gloom above. There was other water too. Moisture could be heard in the walls, disturbing their insect inhabitants.

Duchene and Sabine continued their climb on creaking stairs to the fourth floor. where the corridor was wide enough for just one person. There were no symbols on the doors. Duchene started his count from left to right, then knocked on one of the two doors at the end of the hallway. He heard a grunt from outside.

'Hello?' He called through the door. 'We're friends of Montfort.'

'Voch' aystegh!' called a gruff voice inside.

'Russian?' he mouthed at Sabine.

She shook her head.

Duchene turned and knocked on the other door. There was no response.

He knocked again.

Nothing.

When he tried the handle, it clicked and he slowly pushed the door open. Almost immediately he pulled it shut as the foetid reek hit him. He hunched low, arm across his face, trying to subdue his gag reflex.

Sabine stumbled backwards, her hands to her mouth as she retched.

Duchene managed to stand up. Either the smell was dissipating, or he was becoming more accustomed to it. He braced himself against the wall.

'You don't want to see this.'

'I've seen bodies before.'

'Not like this. Let me look for the money.'

'No. We do it together.'

Sabine wrapped her scarf around her mouth. Duchene did the same and counted to three before pushing the door open again.

Grey light was filtering through the soot-encrusted windows.

One was open, but not enough to diminish the stench of death in the small room. Against one wall was a suitcase, its contents thrown on the floor. There was just enough space to accommodate meagre furnishings – a wash basin and a wire-framed bed. This was where the body lay, across the mattress so that the feet touched the threadbare rug.

Meunier's chest and stomach were a mess of black-brown blood from deep stab wounds. It was hard to distinguish where torn flesh ended and ripped fabric began. The blows had been so fierce that blood was also splattered on the wall behind him and across a little image of a local saint. It had seeped through the thin mattress and dripped onto the floor below. Bed lice were trapped in the gory viscosity like tiny prehistoric creatures in a tar pit.

Duchene, his scarf pressed tightly across his mouth, went over to the window, which had been open for some time, as the sodden wallpaper below it had lifted completely and hung down in damp curls. And it had been forced. The connecting walkway they had seen earlier was just one floor above them. It would be dangerous, but someone could have made it from that to the windowsill of the neighbouring room, then entered this one.

'But if that's how they got in,' Duchene murmured, 'it doesn't make sense that the door was open.'

'How long has he been dead?' Sabine asked, staring at Aaron Meunier's grim face and broken glasses.

'Days.' Duchene said. 'We should go. Quickly. We don't want to be here when the landlady discovers this.'

'Or the police.'

'Exactly.'

'The money?' she said.

'His belongings have been turned over. Someone else has probably taken it.'

'Or maybe they didn't find it.'

Sabine was kneeling on the floor, checking through the scattered clothes and books. Her eyes tracked across the floor.

'What is it?' Duchene asked.

'Someone's moved this rug. This wine stain goes to the edge, but there's a matching stain there, on the floor.'

Duchene offered her his arm and she stood so that they could throw back the rug together. Underneath it, in the centre of floor, a board was missing its nails. Sabine tried to prise it up with her fingers.

'It won't move.'

Duchene offered her his trench knife. She paused to look at the stiletto with its knuckle guard. 'Do you always carry this?'

'Just today. Let's be quick.'

Sabine used the point of the blade to work at the edges of the floorboard, a corner at a time. Shiny beetles scurried out of the light as she picked up a large wad of money.

## Berlin
### Friday, 3 August 1945

# FIFTEEN

He reached the top of the rubble pile. His shins were bruised and his shoes were filling with dust. He sucked in large breaths that strained his lungs and made his chest expand in ways it hadn't in a long time. The sweat from the unaccustomed exertion was beading on his brow and gathering across his back. His discomfort was increased by the beating heat of the sun.

He had long since tucked his linen jacket under one arm and now used the edge of his silk neckerchief to mop his brow.

'It would be great if you could move faster,' Raye called as he and Birgitta scrambled down what remained of an apartment building.

She would have been in her early twenties. Duchene couldn't see much of her father in her face. Her features were less severe and days outdoors with a work gang had dappled her cheeks with freckles. She seemed to read the rubble as she moved, placing each foot with precision, finding those pieces that wouldn't slip away beneath her.

Duchene took one last glance over his shoulder as he crested the pile. Sabine and her men were closing in on the motorcycle. The pile would slow them, but they were moving fast. He quickened his pace, trying to reach Birgitta and follow in her more assured footsteps. Raye was winding his way through archways, paneless windows and door frames. Dust still rained down on them, like an echo of the building's collapse. In other places signs of former lives lay crushed beneath tonnes of stone – the curve of a bath, the flue of a fireplace, the splintered wood of a dining table. And so many hundreds of pages from books that drifted through the wreckage.

Birgitta followed Raye and Duchene followed her. For now, she seemed to be trusting them, or at least hoping they would offer some resistance if the Soviets caught up.

*My enemy's enemy...*

'Here.' From behind the concrete corner of a foundation, Raye offered a water flask to Birgitta.

He had an easy way about him, fluid in his movements despite his size, casual with his smiles and the glances from those dark eyes. Birgitta, only minutes earlier a prisoner, now seemed to accept Raye as her guide. Perhaps, as with so many others who'd survived the war, her instincts had been honed by choices made to maximise her survival, the smile she gave Raye calculated to secure his protection.

Used to rationing, she took only small sips of water, as did Duchene, before passing the flask back to the American.

'You are looking for my father?' she asked in English.

Raye tucked the flask into his pack. He replied in German. 'Once we're safe, we can talk about that. For now we just need to keep up the pace and put some distance between the Russians and us. They're in the French zone, so they won't want to stick around. Not while I have a radio.'

'That woman was asking about him as well. I can tell you the same thing I told her. He's gone. He left when he saw them coming.'

'We've got to keep moving,' Raye said.

As they continued through the maze, he checked his watch. 'There's got to be a patrol around here…'

'Why don't you just radio it in?' Duchene asked.

'It will take too long. My command will need to go through French Command, which will need to send out a patrol, to a position that I don't have because everything around here is blown to shit. But the Russians don't know that. All they see is someone who can call for reinforcements. Let's hope it's enough to send them back to their zone.'

'They'll go where he's going,' Birgitta said.

'How could they know that?' Raye asked.

'I told them. He's looking for a doctor, someone with hydrogen pills.'

'You do understand they're trying to capture him? What they'll do to him when they have him?'

'Why would I hide him? I hate him. My father, Hitler – they've ruined Germany. Good riddance to the Nazis. Look what they've done to us.'

'Bullshit. I'm sure you were there singing along and chanting at all the rallies.' Raye stopped walking. 'You only have a problem with Nazis because they lost the war for you.'

'I was always dissenting.'

'But not that much, or else you wouldn't be alive.'

'I'm not sure if this is helping,' Duchene said. 'Why does he need a doctor? Is he wounded?'

'No. He's trying to get out of Germany.'

The sun was at its height, driving burning rays down onto the ruins. Shadows, at their shortest, gave little relief from the heat. Raye gestured towards a relatively undamaged three-storey building that provided a rare vantage point and Birgitta and Duchene followed him across an empty road.

Inside it was crowded. Women and children sat on the tiled floor or peered down at them from the central stairwell. They were covered in dust, chalk pale against sunburnt skin. Some were eating out of cans, and from somewhere above there came the smell of toast.

'No room,' said an older woman, her hair pulled back in a tight bun. Like so many others, she was well dressed, or would have been, if her hem hadn't been worn to threads.

'We don't want to stay,' Duchene replied in German. 'We only want to rest.'

'These men are Americans,' Birgitta said. 'Soldiers out of uniform.' She pointed to the radio on Raye's back. 'They're needing to call in other Americans, to help. There are Russians in Wedding.'

There was a low murmur around them. Some of the exhausted faces wore scowls of disapproval. Duchene saw one young woman put her face in her hands.

'Fine,' she said. 'Rest. Make your radio call. But don't bring any Russians here.'

'Couldn't agree more, sister,' Raye said under his breath.

Duchene and Birgitta followed Raye as he crossed the foyer and took up a position by one of the windows. A mother with two young boys nodded to him, pulling her blankets out of the way to make space for the radio. Raye set it down, its canvas bottom muffling the thud as it touched the tiles. With the headset in place, he started to move the dials while referring to a notebook in his pocket.

As Duchene sat with his back against the wall, the young woman offered him half an uncooked potato. He shook his head. 'Please, you keep it.'

Birgitta, however, accepted the food and handed Raye's water flask to the children, who sipped as they watched the American work.

'When you mentioned the Russians in Wedding, why did the women react like that?' Duchene asked.

'Only a few of us weren't raped. For me it was four times. In those first weeks, while they were still fighting in the city.' There was no emotion in her voice. 'They dropped flyers from their planes, telling us that we would not be touched. During the day, they were helpful, polite. From farms mostly. But when the night came, they would drink, and bang at our doors or pull us out of our bomb shelters. Their officers, their commissars, they were no help. They said it didn't happen.'

'That's terrible. I'm so sorry.'

'It was what it was. This was back in the time when even our neighbours became our enemies, when we fought over food and stole from one another. That is why I'm glad for the Americans. We can start to rebuild.'

'You speak English well.'

'I learnt it at school. When we began to lose the war, I began to practise. We had a saying, "Optimists learnt English, pessimists learnt Russian.'" She smiled briefly – just punctuation to mark the joke.

'Do you really hate him? Your father?'

'Is that so strange? Do you have children of your own?'

'One. A daughter, and yes, we've had our disagreements, but we could never hate each another. You know what might happen to him? When he stands trial?'

'To me he was always formal, polite. Never loving. As though he was only observing National Socialism's requirement for procreation and childrearing. I was little more than his duty. Which I felt. And I wanted his love, but never got it. So the coldness spreads. But that's not why I hate him, it is because of the war. Because the Russians broadcast news of the death camps and how the Gestapo arrested Jews and hunted them when they hid. How the Nazis tortured and killed the Jews and how they harvested hair and glasses and jewellery. I knew he was part of this. I know he killed civilians.

'But even then, I still did not hate. I was numb. I was confused. I could not believe it. I demanded to know if it was true. And he said nothing. His eyes still righteous. Still defiant. He said nothing to his own daughter, his last living relative. And that was when I understood the stories were true. And that was when the hate grew. So yes, I understand what might happen to him. But he is already dead to me. If he cannot accept his crimes in life, perhaps he will be in hell.'

Raye spoke into the handset of the radio. 'Are you hearing me? This is Captain Raye, OSS officer. Calling in from –' He turned to the room. 'Welche Strasse ist das?'

'Fennstrasse,' someone said.

'Calling in from Fennstrasse, did you get that? Over.'

He held the headset to his ears as he listened to the response. The entire foyer was silent, eyes fixed on Raye.

'That's Fox, Easy, Nan, Nan...Strasse. Over.'

He pulled out his map and held it towards the woman with the children. 'Show me? Ah, zeigen Sie mir bitte?'

The woman pointed to the map.

'Danke. Near the corner of Müllerstrasse. That's Mike, Uncle, Love... You got it? Roger that. It's near a U-Bahn...an underground. Over.'

Raye paused again. 'We've spotted six Red Army in the area. Intelligence probably. Out of uniform. An operation. We need reinforcements – just a show of force. Make that clear. Just flexing some muscle. Can you repeat that back? Over.'

'Roger that. I'll be calling in from a new position soon, but get them to assemble at these coordinates. Over. Oh, and relay this to Major General Bennett. Over and out.'

He flipped a switch on the radio, then turned to Duchene. 'We need to find any doctors nearby that he might have gone to. Damned if I know how. Any ideas?'

Duchene dusted his hands on his pants and hauled himself up.

'Thank you for your hospitality,' he said. 'You've been very patient with us. We've just called for soldiers to come to this building. They'll wait here for us to call. No Russians will come here with the Americans around.'

He felt as though he were back in the classroom with a difficult group of pupils – blank faces stared back at him, giving no indication whether they understood or even cared about what he was saying.

'I have one last favour to ask, please. We need to talk to all the doctors who live nearby. Here in Wedding. It's very important. We will make sure each of them gets one of these,' he said, lifting the medical kit from the floor. 'It's not much but it might help a little.'

---

Outside, Raye kicked a stone across the street.

'Anything else you want to give them? There's a tank back at base we could trade for the names of their dentists. They might have given us the names anyway.'

'You heard what they've been through. I didn't want them to think we were going to hurt their doctors. Besides, I was at Tempelhof. I saw your supplies. What's four medical kits? You'll have enough to spare.'

'Yes, well…'

Drawn in pencil on the map now were four well-separated circles, marking the locations of the remaining doctors in the neighbourhood. It would take them until nightfall to visit them all. Before they'd left Birgitta in the safety of the apartment building, she'd also marked in her old building, where Oberführer Sprenger had been hiding until that morning.

They worked their way past a group of Berliners who were clearing away the remains of a church. They had been provided with wheelbarrows to move the heavy blocks, which were then stacked beside a buttress that still stood.

'Which one do we go to first?'

'The closest one,' Raye said.

'Not the one nearest to where Birgitta was living?'

'We're in a race against the Russians. We have to assume they have the same information as we do. Moving as quickly as possible means we can clear off the two that are closest to our current position. That will cut our list in half.'

'We don't even know if Sprenger will still be there. He's at least two hours ahead of us. He might have moved on.' Duchene was already feeling the tightness in his legs. All his months of limiting how much time he spent on the streets of Paris had made him weak, unused to walking.

'Let's hope the doctor will have some more information. Right now, we're chasing Sprenger's scent. We're just trying to pick it up before the Russkies do.'

'They're not all Russian.'

'Sure, Soviets, then.'

'I think we should work in a different order. If we're assuming they have the same information, we should backtrack – go to the doctor nearest to Birgitta's apartment.'

'And why's that?'

'Because it's what I would have done.'

'Why would the Soviets do what you would have done?' Raye kept moving.

Duchene stopped.

'We can't rest again,' Raye said. 'Come on, Auguste. We get this done and I'll buy all the drinks tonight.'

'You already knew.'

Now Raye stopped.

'Knew what?'

'About Sabine.'

Raye turned. There was no confusion written across his face, not even a smile to distract and redirect the conversation. He simply nodded.

Duchene continued. 'That's why you wanted me so badly. Greer, Bennett, the others... You didn't need me to identify the Oberführer. You had a file on me. In Paris they questioned me about my wife over and over again, about her communism. You wanted me because my wife was leading the Russian team who were also looking for Sprenger.'

Raye held up a hand. 'No, we needed you for both. Sure, we had two other possibilities, another Frenchman and woman, who had been interrogated by Sprenger, but that's the problem with interrogations. It's all the brain can do, trying to help the body survive. Everything else becomes confused and details get missed. You were the best candidate. You have a good mind for detail, you remember faces, you found missing kids in the middle of a goddamn war. And yes, it also helped that your wife was leading the Russians. At some point your knowledge of her might become valuable. Like it has just now.'

Duchene felt the nails pressing into his palms as he tightened his hands into fists. 'When were you going to tell me?'

'Auguste, I'm being honest with you here: we weren't. Unless we needed to, we weren't going to mention it. Keep you focused.'

'I should walk away right now.'

'Why? Other than my deception, which I agree would be upsetting, it doesn't change anything. We're still looking for a war criminal, who we hope will lead us to other war criminals. If the Russians get them, they'll just end up in a mass grave somewhere.

They won't stand trial and the world won't get to hold them to account. To see justice done.'

'She wouldn't execute him.'

'Maybe not her, but she understands what happens next.'

'She's not like that.'

'No? Just take a minute to think beyond her being here in Berlin, beyond my lying, to how she got to be leading a group of Soviet soldiers. The Germans were merciless with the Soviets, brutal. Not just their soldiers, but their civilians as well. The things she would have seen. I'm not saying it makes it right, but you can understand why they raped and pillaged Berlin.'

'There's something else you're hiding,' said Duchene. 'You're trying to distract me. How did you know Sabine was leading the Soviet investigation? How did any of you know?'

'I'm not lying. Promise. We've been setting this up for weeks now, doing our research. There's a lot at stake. We know about Sabine because there's an informant in Soviet intelligence. They're putting their life at risk every time they pass something on to us. That's how we knew about your wife.'

'Another pawn for you to manipulate. Another life to put at risk.'

'It's not my informant. I go via a counterpart in French intelligence. But yes, people get hurt, it's a rough game. You're a reasonable man, Auguste. More reasonable than me. Can we at least keep moving? Be angry while you walk.'

*Informants. Sabine. Him. Their lives at risk.*

Their deaths, his and Sabine's, would be little more than an inconvenience.

'Auguste? Can you please give me the map? It's going to make doubling back to Birgitta's a lot easier.'

Each time Duchene felt he'd identified what was stoking his rage, he turned over another coal and the heat flared up again. He was in Berlin as a result of a deception, because he wouldn't have come if he'd known the truth. Or, more accurately, he would have come but would have been trying to find Sabine, not the Oberführer. This had occurred to him first, this realisation, and he'd finally subsided into a dull anger. Because if the world had learnt one thing from the Nazis, it was how governments and their agents can succeed so much faster through manipulation than truth. And if Duchene knew one thing about the English language, it was that its euphemisms were easily penetrated. The Office of Strategic Services for which Raye worked meant spying, or sabotage, or assassination – the things you did when you didn't want to follow the Geneva Convention.

But his new rage, growing now inside him, was directed at Sabine. Because Raye had been right: he hadn't put any thought into how she had become a military leader in the Red Army. And putting aside the crash of deeply troubling ideas that Raye had just thrown at him, he also realised that she hadn't done a thing, from her position of power, to let him know that she was alive and well.

'Still working through it all?' Raye used his shirt sleeve to mop his forehead.

Duchene said nothing.

'How about this, then – tell me why she would be going to this doctor and not the others?'

'Start at the beginning.' Duchene could hear the anger in his voice. 'It's something I told her once.'

'Before the war?'

'Back in Paris, before she left for Spain. She was a forewoman in a car and bicycle factory. I helped her to investigate a murder.'

'Murder? You'll have to tell me about that one.' Raye checked his watch. 'It'll be evening soon. We'd better push on. Are you keeping up?'

Duchene didn't even have the energy to nod. His shirt was soaked through and his feet ached. His whole body felt as though it was trembling.

Raye took something from his pocket. 'Here,' he said, handing Duchene a box, 'if you're hungry.'

Tropical Chocolate from someone called Hershey.

'Thank you. You don't want it?' Once unwrapped, the dense bar, dark and hard, looked nothing like chocolate.

'Had more of them than I can stand. The boys like to call it Hitler's secret weapon.' Raye passed Duchene his knife. 'You'll have to shave pieces off to eat it.'

Raye glanced at Duchene's face as he put some in his mouth. 'Bad, isn't it?'

As they moved on, however, Duchene ate a little more. It was bitter and gritty, but at least distracted him from the pain that stirred with every step. He searched for a landmark he could use to orient himself, something that would make him confident they were drawing closer to Birgitta's apartment. He found nothing. Where Berlin once had architecture it now had open sky.

The rubble picking had stopped for the day and now street life turned to new activity. Old men, women and children were carrying water and gathering wood from neatly stacked piles of timber in order to light fires and cook a rough meal. Duchene had seen a few ration queues throughout the day, the thin bodies inching forward, then taking away some meagre allowance of bread or fat or coffee substitute.

Raye, ahead of him, map in hand, was looking up at a rare street sign. 'This way!' He started to run.

Duchene increased his pace, regretting every footfall, as he followed the American around the corner and into a small plaza. Here there were habitable buildings, burnt and shelled, but mostly standing. A young girl was playing the violin alongside an elderly cellist, their bows moving in time as they filled the square with music. The remnants of families were preparing food around the edges of the square while others watched from the windows of the buildings. Raye stared around him. 'Okay, so we're in the right place. Let's ask.'

'No need,' Duchene said. 'Look.'

He pointed to the ground floor of a building distinguished from those above it by the presence of windows. Or, at least, what stood in for windows. Where the glass had been shattered, large radiograph slides had been used to replace them. In the shadow of the building, x-ray bones of Berliners stood on display, their femurs, ribs and hips dimly backlit from the clinic inside.

Duchene scanned the square, which was growing busier as night neared and children were calmed with the comforting ritual of stories they had known when their apartments were still whole. Raye was doing the same, his dark eyes moving quickly over the crowd.

'See them?'

'No,' Duchene replied, though he wasn't looking for a 'them' but rather a 'her'. He didn't doubt that if Sabine were present, she'd be taking care not to be seen by him. Perhaps he should follow her example.

'We need to establish if Sprenger's in there,' Raye said, removing the backpack and pulling a gun from one of its canvas pockets. He slipped this into the waistband of his trousers before taking out the second gun and offering it to Duchene.

'I'll be fine.'

'Not with a bullet in your head you won't. If Sprenger is in there he won't be unarmed and he won't be happy to see us. How long do you think it will take for him to put it together, seeing you in Berlin?'

'Not long. We should make sure he doesn't see us.'

Raye shook his head. 'We don't have control over this situation. I'd feel better, for both of us, if you were armed.'

'I wouldn't. It's been a long time since I fired a pistol. I'm just as likely to accidentally kill him as disable him.'

Raye sighed and returned the weapon to the pack. 'Pass me your jacket.'

Raye draped it over the top of the radio, which he now carried in his left hand rather than on his back. It was cumbersome, and he strained under the weight. In any other circumstances, this would have stood out to even a casual observer, but this was post-war Berlin where impractical heirlooms were carried across rubble by failing arms and tiring legs.

Raye gestured at Duchene and then towards the right window of the clinic. He motioned to himself and then to the left window. Duchene nodded and they separated.

He reached the wall and leant his back against it, making his best efforts to appear as though he was taking a rest. It didn't require much by way of deception. His muscles ached. Raye was observing the same caution, hunched down by the window and tying his shoelace. In a city emerging from a war, doctors were highly prized and strange activity outside their offices would be noticed. Duchene placed one foot against the wall and lit a cigarette. Turning his head sideways, he reached a finger to the corner of one of the x-rays and lifted it just enough to see into the room.

It was lit by a few scavenged bulbs, their feeble light reinforced with two Hindenburg lights, flames flickering on fat wicks in the centre of molten tallow. Mismatched shelves had been placed against a scorched wall. They were largely empty, containing only a few medical jars and containers. Laundered rags were placed to one side, ready to be used as bandages. Equipment was laid out on a small table beside a barber's chair that stood in for an operating table. This was where Oberführer Sprenger sat.

Shirtless, he held a gun in his right hand while a grey-haired woman in a baker's apron bent over his left arm. Duchene couldn't see what she was doing, but her movements were small and precise.

Though his face had lost its jowly softness and his shaved hair was almost the same length as the grey stubble on his face, the man's eyes were the same – dark, focused and exacting. The eyes of the man who'd questioned him at Gestapo headquarters in Paris.

Duchene let the x-ray fall back into position and looked across to Raye, who was taking up a position next to a burnt-out car.

The musicians finished their piece to applause and moved on to a rendition of Glenn Miller's 'Moonlight Serenade' – the warm, gentle notes filled the air.

Duchene hurried over to Raye. 'He's in there. With the doctor. We need to get her out of there.'

'Too hard. He'll start shooting if we storm the place, but with ricochets, her being so close to him, those windows, these people – too easy for something to go wrong.'

'So we wait?'

Raye nodded. 'Try and grab him on his way out.'

'And what about them?' Duchene indicated the smiling Germans, their eyes on the performers.

'I'll try to explain what we're doing. You heard his daughter, she's not alone in hating the Nazis.'

The throbbing in Duchene's feet reminded him of only three nights earlier, as he ran from vigilantes through the Paris streets.

'Will they try to hang him?'

'I wouldn't think so. I reckon they'll just keep their heads down and let us go about our business. I'll radio it in and get the truck to redeploy a block from here, out of sight. Once we have him, I'll call it in and they can meet us.'

'What do you need me to do?'

Raye placed the radio at Duchene's feet. 'Keep this with you.' He shoved his gun into Duchene's hand. 'And this. Keep an eye on the door. You need to stop him if he leaves.'

The weight of the automatic pistol surprised Duchene. Its hard edges pressed into his hand and he resisted the urge to turn it so that its brown plastic grip sat more comfortably.

'You've used a semi-automatic before?'

'No. But I've seen how it's done – pull back the slide.'

'Exactly. Pulling the trigger will do the rest.'

Raye began to jog towards a collapsed apartment at the edge of the square. 'Stay here, I'll get back to you on the double.'

Duchene bundled his neckerchief around the pistol and held it at his side. Facing the clinic door, he continued to smoke his cigarette. He hadn't been on watch for very long when he heard a young child's voice. A little boy, wearing only a shirt and shorts, was wandering barefoot through the crowd.

'Mutti?' His voice was too soft to be heard over the music. 'Mutti?' His small feet shuffled on the ground, uncertain of where to turn.

Duchene tucked the gun into the back of his trousers. He beamed at the toddler and squatted down in front of him.

'Are you looking for your mummy?' he asked in German.

The little boy stared back at him, unsure, worried.

'Your mummy?'

Duchene looked around. The child couldn't have wandered far. He offered his kerchief, lifting it and letting it float down like a parachute. 'See how it falls?'

The little boy reached out for it.

Many in the crowd were still absorbed by the musicians. Others were listening as they carried out their tasks. Then Duchene saw her. A woman moving through those near the performers, her face harried, her eyes moving rapidly. He held up his hand.

'Thank you. Thank you.' She swept in and lifted the boy into her arms. He immediately burst into tears, as his tension was released. 'I'm so sorry he bothered you.'

'Not at all. Mine was always wandering off at this age.'

'Here,' she said, trying to prise the kerchief from the boy's hands.

'Please, no. Let him keep it,' Duchene said.

'We can't.'

'I insist.'

'That's very kind of you,' the mother said. 'Thank you.'

Duchene watched as she stepped sideways around a tightly packed group of men and disappeared towards whatever passed for her home.

He glanced back at the men. Clean shaven. Soldiers' boots a mismatch for civilian clothes. And at their centre, Sabine.

*Sabine*.

The Russians were scanning the square, looking up to the apartments and assessing as he and Raye had done minutes earlier. There were more people now standing in front of the buildings; perhaps they would take longer to see the x-rays.

'You made a friend,' Raye said as he arrived at Duchene's side.

'The Russians,' Duchene whispered, even though the music and distance would make it impossible for them to be heard.

'Shit. We go now.' Raye drew his gun and started to walk quickly. Duchene could see the American's body tighten, straining against a desire to break into a full run.

'What about the doctor?'

'What about us? We're not in control of this situation. We just have to hope she's lucky. Take the radio, go to the door, knock. When you hear my call, come in.'

'What are you going to do?'

'Just do it!'

Duchene grabbed and hurried inside, pushing himself against

the wall to pass an old woman struggling with a charred branch she was using as a walking stick. A corridor led towards a flight of stairs and along one side were three green doors, the first bearing a painted image of two serpents twined around a winged staff. Someone had taken their time with the image – a first step in the return to civility. Duchene could see that the second and third doors had once been painted too. The word 'Quarantäne' had been scrubbed off the green paint, leaving only a faded impression behind.

Duchene paused at the door, held his ear against the wood. All he could hear was the sound of the doctor moving across the floor. Then came a crash.

'Stop!' Raye was shouting in German. 'Don't move!'

Duchene had only a second to form an impression once he was through the door. Light from the setting sun bathed the room in a warm glow. Raye had crashed through the x-rays, which were now gathered at his feet, leaving an entire window open to the square outside. Sprenger was still in the chair with the doctor at his side.

In an eruption of movement, the three men behaved as though they were pieces in a game of speed chess, taking moves, making rapid calculations, moving again.

Sprenger swung his Luger from Raye to Duchene as the American stepped forward and pulled the doctor back towards him. Her movements were slow, confused. Duchene felt his breathing stop as the gun's attention was drawn to him.

Standing quickly, Sprenger put his back to the wall, reducing his exposure, while Raye stepped in front of the doctor, using his body as a shield. The German now had the Luger trained on him.

As Duchene pushed the door closed with his foot, Sprenger

swung his pistol back briefly, his eyes widening before he faced Raye once again.

'Monsieur Duchene, they've brought you to Berlin to identify me.' Sprenger spoke in French.

'Wouldn't seem that was needed,' Duchene replied, 'since you've identified yourself.'

'And you're still hunting men, more successfully this time. How good for you. There are very few people who are still alive who know me. How did you find me?'

'One of your henchmen – Allmann.'

'I wouldn't have thought it possible to be a traitor twice over. But there you have it. And this man here, an American soldier? He's the one holding the dog's leash?'

'I'm the one holding a gun,' Raye replied in French. 'Drop your weapon and come peacefully.'

'Come peacefully? But for how long? Or are we suggesting that an execution, if it's decided by a sham trial, is no longer violent?'

'Not a sham. An international court. For war criminals. You can make your case, for all the good it will do you.'

Duchene was very aware of the time it was taking to resolve this stand-off. If the Russians hadn't already realised the location of the clinic, they would have done so the moment Raye had thrown himself through the makeshift window. The music was still playing outside.

'Quickly, please. Put the window back up,' Duchene said to the doctor.

She regarded him with caution.

'So no one out there gets hurt,' he continued.

She nodded and began to replace the x-rays in the window

frame, taping them together. A few onlookers had come forward to see what had happened.

'It's nothing,' she said. Her voice had the deep timbre that comes from years of smoking. 'Just a little too much to drink. He fell through.'

'Lucky him,' one of the onlookers called. 'Does he have any more?'

There was laughter.

Duchene could see at least one of the Russians, barely an adult, perhaps seventeen, jogging towards them.

'The Russians are getting close,' Duchene said in English. 'We need to get him out of here.'

'A bit too hard right now to radio in a call,' Raye replied. Raye was shifting sideways, trying to keep himself between the Luger and the doctor.

The Oberführer's grip tightened on the pistol.

'Russians…' he said in English, then put the gun under his chin and pulled the trigger.

The ringing of the gunshot saved Duchene from hearing the wet sound of brain matter splattering on the wall behind Sprenger. He also managed to turn his face away, so that he caught only a glimpse of the red and pink erupting from the top of the man's head. But he wasn't saved from the smell, the sudden coppery burst that filled the room. Duchene's stomach seized, but with little food in there, he merely retched.

'Fuck!' Raye shouted.

The body twitched, the blood was pooling and Duchene found himself looking at the spray of red that now clung to the wall and ceiling.

'Fuck'n asshole,' Raye said, dragging the radio into the room and dropping to the floor. Duchene joined him by the window and peeled back one of the x-rays.

'What now?'

The men and women closest to the clinic were crouched on the ground, hands over their heads, eyes searching for where the shot had come from. From them there radiated a ripple of reaction, first to those who had half-heard the sound, and were still uncertain if it wasn't imagined, to those nearest the musicians who heard nothing, and then finally the violinist and cellist, who were still playing.

The gunshot had, however, revealed the Russians – four young men in caps, despite the heat, who had just drawn pistols. Sabine, Duchene saw, was close behind the men and had not drawn a weapon. She had removed her cap and her hair fell in black waves to her shoulders. After glancing in his direction, she moved into the crowd. The Russians were taking up positions facing the clinic.

'Do we wave a white flag?'

'No, we fight them,' Raye said, finding his frequency and picking up the receiver. 'It's Captain Raye. I need you to come to me at the end of the square. This is a fire order. We have five armed Russians moving in our position. Over.'

The Germans were starting to edge away from the armed men who, bent low, were heading for the clinic. Then from one corner of the square appeared an American military truck. All eyes turned, and the musicians stopped playing, as it rolled over the cobblestones.

It was obvious that the Russians' confidence was falling away;

their faces were setting into expressions of grim resignation. They pulled the slides on their pistols and locked eyes with the truck.

'The Americans won't shoot at them?' asked Duchene.

'Only if they're too stupid to drop their weapons.'

'And risk a war with the USSR?'

'They're not dressed as Russians. We'd be firing on men we understood to be insurgents.'

Duchene searched for Sabine and saw her, beside the cellist. She said something in his ear, then handed him several packets of cigarettes. He nodded, spoke to the violinist and counted her in.

It was a tango, dynamic and passionate. Sabine held out her hand to a man beside her and pulled him into the centre of the square. His steps were awkward, but he grinned at her as they turned in tight circles. Others soon started to fill the makeshift dance floor.

As American soldiers piled out of the back of the truck, the Russians concealed their pistols and drifted back among the dancers.

Raye was with the Americans now, pointing and shouting orders, but they had lost the Russians in the swirl and motion of the dancing around them.

Duchene couldn't help but smile.

## SIXTEEN

'It's not funny,' Raye said as Duchene handed back the pistol.

'Which part? I agree there's nothing funny about a dead man who's no longer able to stand trial.'

'I've spent enough time around you to know what's going through that brain of yours. You're impressed by her.'

'She's my wife. I'm allowed to be impressed by her.'

They were sitting outside the clinic as American and French soldiers walked about the square, handing out chocolate and trying to establish where the Russians might have disappeared to. It seemed obvious to Duchene – outnumbered and without a target, Sabine would have pulled her team back across to the Soviet zone.

He picked up the medical kit from beside Raye and waved it meaningfully.

'Sure...fine. There'll be a few in the back of the truck. I'll get one of the boys to bring them over.'

Duchene knocked on the open door of the clinic.

'At least you enter in a more civilised way this time,' the doctor said.

'Sorry about that. My colleague, he's a little hot-headed when it comes to war criminals.'

'Hot-headed? That's one way to describe it.'

She had covered the Oberführer's body with a mouldy blanket and was using a rag to clean the blood from the walls. Two women were helping her, their hands dipping in and out of the spent artillery shells they were using as buckets.

Duchene held out the medical kit. 'For you. To help the people. I'm Auguste.'

'Helene Scheidecker,' she replied.

'That's not a German name.'

'Swiss,' she said. 'May I also have one of your cigarettes?'

Duchene took one for himself and gave her the rest of the packet.

'Did he say much when he was here?'

'Very little. Just asked me to remove the tattoo on his arm. So I used hydrogen pills and rubbed their contents on the skin. It would have been raw for a few days, but once it was healed the tattoo would have been gone.'

'What was it?'

'His blood type.'

Duchene lit their cigarettes. A private arrived, carrying three more medical kits. Scheidecker gestured to the empty shelves on the wall.

'The Americans will remove his body,' Duchene said.

'Will he be buried?'

'I'm not sure. He was a war criminal, Gestapo, SS. I think they'll probably cremate him. Are you sure he didn't say anything else, about meeting with someone? We're looking for the head of the Gestapo, Heinrich Müller. Trying to bring him to the Hague war trials.'

'I'm afraid not.'

'Well, thank you for your time.'

As Scheidecker led him back into the corridor, Duchene looked again at the faded writing on the door.

'What did you have to quarantine against? Typhus?'

'The Russians,' she replied.

## Saturday, 4 August 1945

## SEVENTEEN

The coffee was strong, but still too watery for Duchene. As far as he was concerned, Americano had always sounded like an excuse, not a preference. An excuse for failing to understand that a coffee should be small and bitter and drunk in a few sips. Maybe this was the beginning of a new decline as American culture spread throughout Europe. Or perhaps the Americans were what was needed. Two brutal wars in the span of thirty years didn't suggest Europe was at the peak of civilisation.

Duchene sat on a small leather settee in Andrews Barracks. Eyes closed, he took another sip of coffee, listening to the hive buzz of the morning's activity, from the clatter of typewriters and teletype printers to the burble of conversation. A new sound, the clack of approaching heels, caused him to open his eyes.

First Sergeant Davis arrived at his side.

'Do you need anything else from the mess? I can call for a steward,' she said.

Her uniform was, like that of everyone in the building, except perhaps Captain Raye, clean and crisp and pressed and would stand an inspection. A contrast to the streets of Berlin where GIs had a broader interpretation of regulations. Even this morning, as he stood waiting in the heat for Corporal Austin to arrive with the jeep and a whole cabbage for Ernest, he had seen young GIs stripping down to their briefs and dog tags to dive into the black water of the canal opposite the hotel.

Duchene shook his head. 'No thank you.'

She smiled briefly and indicated to the door beside her. 'They're ready for you.'

In Bennett's office the same people sat in almost the same positions as the last time he'd been here, as though they'd been waiting the entire time for his return. Bennett was in the centre, his barrel body filling most of the settee. To his left was Leterrier, lean and upright on the edge of the armchair, while, to his right, Wright lounged deep into his chair, his ankles crossed and his hands poised in a steeple in front of his face. Greer sat on the arm of the second settee, which was already occupied by a uniformed Raye, who moved sideways to make a space for Duchene.

'Mr Duchene. Do you need anything? Another coffee?'

'No, thank you.' Duchene noted that he was the only one with a drink of any kind.

'Very good. Let's jump right in. We need you to keep backing us here in Berlin.'

'I'm not sure what that means, General?'

'It's not over,' Greer said.

'You're talking about Heinrich Müller?' Duchene asked.

'If in the process of your investigation you come across information as to his whereabouts it would be gratefully received,' Wright said. 'However, SS-Oberführer Volker Sprenger was never the primary target of your investigation. Before Berlin fell, we had a German informant working for us, who passed on information about a box file that Sprenger carried with him. It contained Russian schematics obtained during his interrogation of an Austrian resistance group.'

'Schematics?'

'We need them for the war effort,' Leterrier said. 'Japan hasn't surrendered and –'

'Excuse me, Colonel, but I believe what you intended to say was that you need to keep them away from the Russians,' Duchene said.

Bennett sat forward in his chair, shoulders squared and his expression intent.

'Well, alright then. Let's talk more directly.' Bennett glanced at the British officer. 'Brigadier Wright, could you brief Mr Duchene?'

'We had to consider the classified nature of these schematics, and their potential value to our governments. You can appreciate that we didn't disclose this to you when we first briefed you. Oberführer Sprenger may be dead but we still need to find those documents.'

'Keep them away from the Russians.'

'Exactly.'

'That's why they were so determined to capture the Oberführer. Why they crossed into the French zone.'

Wright tapped his steepled fingers on his chin. 'Although the agreement is yet to be formally signed, it's understood that we won't be conducting military operations in one another's territories. Not the best way to keep the peace between us.'

'I thought they were our allies?'

'I think it's safe to say we're beginning to retreat from that understanding. The goal here is to try and not hasten its decline.' Wright looked directly at Raye.

'Respectfully, sir, we didn't shoot any of them.'

'But you did call in a rifle squad. We're just lucky no shots were actually fired at the Russians yesterday. That is correct, Captain?'

Duchene watched as Raye nodded back, without a single tell or movement beyond what was absolutely necessary. 'That is correct, Brigadier, sir.'

Wright continued. 'I had been advised that discretion was one of your main attributes, Captain Raye.'

Greer scratched his head behind the scarred mess of what had been his left ear. 'You have a point, sir, but Raye is one of my best men. He's operating under pressure in a difficult environment. If you want success, and fast, discretion isn't always possible.'

'I'm sure we've all had to break more than we'd like to complete a mission,' Bennett said.

The corners of Leterrier's mouth tightened, as if at a bad memory.

'The revised objective,' Wright continued, 'is to assist Captain Raye to find these documents. He has a description of the container they were in and where they were last seen.'

'I'm not sure if I can help,' Duchene said.

'Then you will try.' Leterrier pointed at one of the three manila folders on the coffee table. 'You will try because that is your duty to France and to our allies. As long as the Soviets are still hunting for the schematics, we're still hunting for the schematics.'

'You mean as long as my wife is still running their investigation, you want me around while you run yours? What's in these schematics that means you need to stop the Russians from getting them back?'

'That's classified,' Wright said.

'You do realise that *if* I find them, I might end up seeing them.'

'General, he has a point,' Raye said. 'It's better that Monsieur Duchene understands what's at risk here.'

Bennett looked at his companions, 'Colonel? Brigadier?'

'Agreed,' Leterrier said. Wright inclined his head.

'They're schematics for a long-range guided ballistic missile,' Bennett said

'The Russians have been seizing rockets and materials around Germany,' Greer said. 'We're trying to limit their ability to build their own versions of the rockets.'

'Are you building the rockets?' Duchene asked.

The brigadier spoke calmly, his fingers stretched on the leather arms of his chair. 'Mr Duchene, we are in a race against the Soviets. Stalin has shown he is unwilling to cede the countries the Red Army occupied. This is a new threat to the stability of the world.'

'We need you to help us to slow his ambitions,' Bennett said.

'It is a simple question. We have given you as much time as we are willing,' Leterrier said.

Duchene picked up the coffee from the table. It was cold, but he sipped at it anyway. The information was still rolling over him, yet to flatten to a calm he could interpret and digest. Would they even let him go back to Paris if he refused? The Soviets and the Americans were only going to push harder, now that Sprenger was dead. Sabine might be a willing participant in this race, but she, too, was at risk of being ground under by the nations that were running it.

*Sabine.*

'What can I can do to help?'

## EIGHTEEN

'So what do we do now?' Raye said as he lit a cigarette and placed his feet on the table.

They had been given their own room on the second floor of the administration building, though Duchene was struggling to see its purpose. Aside from a table and the two chairs they were sitting on, it contained only a cratered cork board to which a German map of central Berlin was pinned. The map still bore a swastika on each corner and its locations were shown in the heavy Gothic font used by the Nazis.

'Duchene?' Raye said again.

'I don't know. Ask some questions? Start to try to unpick the knot.'

'The knot?'

'It's all there, somewhere. We might not be able to see it, might never see it. But we have some information.'

'Okay, this is good.' Raye sat up and pulled his notepad out of his pocket.

'We have the Oberführer. He was at the doctor having a tattoo of his blood type removed. Why?'

'That we know. Most SS have them tattooed on their left arm.

So they could still get medical treatment without their dog tags. It's how we've been catching them.'

'So why did he choose to leave now? Why not earlier?'

'We don't know. We found some fake papers in his clothes when we brought his body back to camp last night. Fake passport and a thousand Reichsmarks.'

'Maybe it took him time to pull it all together?'

'Maybe.'

'Then, let's go back to the last time he was seen.'

'That was on the fifteenth of April, when he was in Gestapo HQ during the RAF bombing raids.' Raye picked up a file. 'That was the last time we knew he had the schematics.'

'Can we talk to this German informant?'

'She's dead, unfortunately. Executed by the Gestapo. She'd been asked to retrieve the schematics. Never made it out.'

'I'm sorry.'

'I'd never met her. Must have been brave.'

'I'm assuming these Gestapo headquarters are in the Soviet zone. Or else you would have searched them.'

'Yes.' Raye stood and stuck a pin in the map. 'On Prinz-Albrecht-Strasse, close to the border between the US and Soviet zones.'

Duchene stood to look at the map that no longer bore any resemblance to the Berlin in which they now stood. The web of streets that ran out from the Mitte at the centre of the city, the U-Bahns marked in rectangles, the Spree and its canals, even its parks and gardens, blasted by tanks and heavy artillery.

'What about Allmann? You said he was picked up trying to cross the Elbe having come from Gestapo headquarters. Perhaps he knows something else?'

'We already spoke to him. He gave us everything he had.'

'He gave you everything he had on the Oberführer. Did you ask him about the schematics?'

Raye grabbed his jacket from the back of the chair. 'I'll get a jeep.'

---

Raye wore a pair of aviator glasses to cut the glare of the day as he drove.

'How can you be so sure Allmann and the others will still be at the camp?' Duchene shouted.

'It's been less than forty-eight hours since I signed off on sending them back to the field camps. Usually takes two days to requisition a boxcar and another day to get a train to bring it from the Rhein. And that's if everything goes to plan. Took me the better part of a week to get them up to Berlin in the first place.'

'Let's hope he knows something.'

'Agreed.'

'Did you know about the schematics? Yesterday, when we were searching for the doctor, when I caught you in a lie about Sabine, you said you'd told me everything you knew.'

'I didn't know about the schematics.'

Raye pulled the jeep onto the side of the road, bringing it to a sudden stop in front of the scorched turret of a Russian tank. He let the vehicle idle while he turned to face Duchene and removed his sunglasses. His brow was furrowed and there were dark rings under the eyes that looked directly into Duchene's.

'Auguste, I didn't know about the schematics.'

'Alright.

'You have to believe me.'

'Does it matter?'

Raye slapped a hand on the steering wheel. 'It does. Listen. I thought there was something else going on but they didn't tell me. I'm not stupid – I know we wouldn't throw these sorts of resources at hunting a mid-ranked officer. Even if he was a war criminal. I didn't tell you because we needed to concentrate on what we were doing, not speculate.'

When Raye had lied to his superiors about firing on Russian soldiers, it had come easily and without those small signs that Duchene had come to look for. No eye movement, no finger twitch, no shift to reposition the body as the question was asked. Even now Raye's eyes were locked on Duchene's.

'You believe me?'

Now it was Duchene's turn to sell the lie. 'I believe you.'

'Great!' Raye shifted the clutch and thrust them back out onto the road.

In only a few more minutes they were following the line of linden trees that led to the turn-off to the camp. Duchene was immediately taken back to the other night. Raye's right hand was still bruised from the beating he'd given the Gestapo.

'Last time we were here, when you interrogated him, you told me he wasn't a prisoner of war. Because, what? He's a war criminal?'

'No,' Raye said, slowing as they reached the gates. 'Because that's not his designation. Captured Germans are disarmed enemy forces.'

'And what is the difference?'

'Nazi Germany no longer exists as a state, so the Geneva Convention doesn't apply to them.'

The gates of the camp were open. Only one soldier stood on guard. Inside the compound a line of men was queuing beside the bunkhouse. The strong smell of a meaty stew was carried towards them on the breeze.

Raye snatched the glasses from his face. The jeep had barely stopped before he was out and running towards the administration building.

Duchene looked more carefully at the line of men. There were fewer of them than there had been the other day and though their clothes were still in disarray, he could see the olive green trousers, the tan service boots, the mustard shirts.

Duchene reached the office in time to see Raye slamming his hand on a field table. 'You're fucking kidding me!'

The young sergeant he was speaking to was red faced, though more from shock, perhaps, than embarrassment. The office was obviously temporary, set up with collapsible chairs and tables, ready to be decamped in minutes. Although it had been cleaned of all debris and the windows patched, the room had the faint ammonia smell of animal urine.

'I'm sorry, Captain, but these orders were signed off by General Bradley, delivered just after zero nine hundred. We didn't bring it to your attention because you'd already signed the paperwork to return the prisoners to the Rhein camps.'

'I signed orders that would still have them in our custody.'

'The men in the camp are Americans, not Germans,' Duchene said.

'So I've just been told. Damnit!' Raye stormed towards the

door, then stopped, his hand on the handle. 'How long since they left?'

'Forty minutes ago,' the sergeant replied. 'Three trucks, sir, and six jeeps.'

'More than enough time to get back into the Soviet zone,' Raye said.

'What's happened?' Duchene asked.

'The Russians made a deal with the Control Group Council to exchange the Gestapo for US soldiers liberated from ex-German work camps.'

'The Germans surrendered two months ago,' Duchene said. 'The Soviets are saying they only just found them?'

Raye leant against the door jamb and crossed his arms. 'What was the word, Sergeant?'

'*Processed*, sir. They only just finished processing them.'

Duchene shook his head. 'You have to wonder.'

'Yes, the timing is fucking convenient.'

'And Allmann?'

'Gone.' Raye pushed off the wall and threw the door open. 'The Russians have him now.'

# PARIS
## Sunday, 15 November 1936

# NINETEEN

'Put the money in here.' Duchene grabbed a shirt off the floor and passed it to Sabine.

'If we're carrying clothes out of the room, won't it attract the landlady's attention?'

'Better than a bundle of cash. Better than getting bed lice.'

'Good point. I'll put it under my coat.' Sabine replaced the floorboard and pulled the rug back over it.

The longer he spent here, the more Duchene felt that the smell of death would become a part of him. He could feel its odour collecting in the recesses of his nose, gathering in his clothing and settling into his hair. A dead man lay less than a metre from him. A life that had been was no more. But these sympathies were purely intellectual. His stomach roiled from the smell – the sick, sweet smell of decay that fed into animal instincts of repulsion and flight.

Duchene forced himself to take in the room once more. Aaron Meunier, stabbed on the bed. Still in his day clothes, his coat spread open around him, his pockets turned out. His shoes removed, then tossed to one side. Their laces had been untied and the tongues lifted.

'We need to go,' Sabine said.

'Just a moment.' Duchene tracked the clothes across the floor, back to the open suitcase, now empty, its linings cut open. Duchene examined it. The luggage label stickers showed recent ports it had been through – Calais and Oslo and Le Havre.

'His passport. Quick, can you see it anywhere?'

Sabine rummaged through the clothes, then turned back the flaps of Meunier's coat.

'Auguste,' she said.

It was loose, sitting on a dried pool of blood.

'That's been placed there.' As he lifted a corner of the passport from the bloody mess, using a handkerchief that had been lying on the floor, the cover ripped. Duchene wrapped the passport and placed it in his pocket; Sabine did the same with the stack of francs.

He pulled the door shut and they started towards the stairs. 'You go first,' said Duchene.

'Did you give him my message?' The landlady's question went unanswered as Duchene and Sabine moved quickly past and out into the alleyway.

As soon as they were no longer in her sightline, they began to run, slowing to a walk only once they were back on the street.

Sabine was catching her breath, her voice hoarse as she spoke. 'We should take this back to the party office. Right away.'

'I agree. It's too much to carry around. We don't want to end up like Vincent or Meunier.'

The rain had eased to light showers, slicking the streets so that the headlamps of automobiles reflected on stones and windows.

As they turned another corner, Sabine glanced over her shoulder to see if they were being followed.

'Anyone?'

'No.'

After the cold wind in the streets, the Métro felt damp and humid. Some of the framed advertising posters on the tiled walls promised unattainable luxury – a car racing along a Cote d'Azur boulevard – but others offered more affordable glamour: an hour or two at the cinema with a smoky-eyed Marlene Dietrich.

A rush of wind heralded the arrival of the train, tugging at newspapers and the edges of coats. After sliding open the wooden door, Sabine held it open for two elderly men before she and Duchene stepped into the carriage. The bulbs that lined the roof flickered and, with a hiss, the train resumed its journey.

As Sabine leant her head on his shoulder, Duchene drew in the smell of her, the citrusy perfume that was slowly fading, the chalkiness of the make-up she used sparingly so that it would last. But under these was her true smell – the faint scent of the ocean and the earthiness of clay, those essential minerals that made up her unique chemistry.

Sabine spoke softly into his ear. 'What were you doing back there? Why did you wait after we found the money?'

'I was trying to take in as much of it as I could.'

'Why?'

'To understand why he was killed.'

She lifted her head from his shoulder. His words seemed to summon her own recollection of the room.

'And did you? Understand?'

'I have a theory. Because of what was left behind and what was taken.'

'Taken?'

'Montfort said he hadn't heard from Meunier, not since he left for Paris.'

'You asked him if he'd show us his letter. He became flustered.'

'Meunier had come from Norway.'

'Ah, the labels on his suitcase.'

'Yes – Oslo. If we look at the dates in his passport it will confirm it. But Montfort tried to hide his deceptions in a half-truth. He wasn't just afraid about his and Meunier's safety because of the persecution of Trotsky and his followers. It was because of something they were doing here and now.'

'Trotsky's in Norway, under house arrest. Do you think Meunier was carrying a letter to Paris Trotskyists from their leader?'

'I do.'

'So the room wasn't turned over in search of the money. They were looking for the letter?'

'Yes, probably in the shoes, because you wouldn't start your search there. But that's not what concerns me, what doesn't make sense. The way the rug matched up with the wine stain suggests it was moved before the room was turned over. That means the room would have been clean when the killer arrived.'

Sabine chuckled. 'I'm not sure if anyone could have ever called that room clean.'

'If I was the killer,' Duchene continued, 'after I stabbed Meunier, and I was looking for the letter, why didn't I make that same connection? Why didn't I lift the rug and discover the money?'

'Perhaps you didn't see it.

'Possibly. Maybe the killer moved straight to searching the body, then the case, then removed the shoes. That's the order in my mind. By throwing the contents of the suitcase around the room, they made it harder to see the rug had been removed.'

'Well, it's a good thing they didn't.'

'The Central Committee, what will they make of this Trotsky connection?' asked Duchene.

'Thorez and his faction support global Soviet communism and agree with Trotsky's exile, but their main concern is finding new members for the PCF and, of course, the war in Spain. I'd always have picked Langlois, not Vincent, as a closet Trotskyist. He probably hoped Trotsky would seize power, not Stalin. And he's the one who put us in contact with Montfort. We should tell them what we've discovered.'

❧

'You're saying that Vincent met Aaron Meunier and gave him the money?'

They had spent the last ten minutes explaining to the Central Committee what had happened at the boarding house and Bloyer had seized on the one piece of the puzzle that eluded Duchene.

'That…I'm not so sure,' Duchene replied. 'Perhaps Vincent gave him the money, Meunier hid it and then was murdered.'

'And this killer, or killers, also murdered Comrade Vincent?' Langlois asked.

Though a quorum of the Central Committee had been hurriedly assembled in the top-floor meeting room, Langlois and

Bigarde led the questions. Duchene and Sabine stood at the head of the table; the committee sat around it; the money lay in the centre.

'The only thing that would suggest that is the connection with Meunier and the money being in his room. It's possible, but I wouldn't say it's certain.'

'It seems very likely,' Langlois said.

Discomfort became visible as the men shifted in their chairs.

'Not enough to satisfy me,' Duchene said. 'There are a number of unanswered questions.'

'Such as?' Bigarde asked.

'Who killed Vincent.'

'That's possibly a delicate matter,' Langlois said.

'Because they might have been acting on behalf of Stalin, the NKVD,' Duchene said.

The murmur increased into raised voices of dissatisfaction.

'Be very cautious about what you're suggesting, Monsieur Duchene,' Bigarde said, his voice lifting above the noise.

'Comrades, comrades.' Bloyer held out his hands. 'We mustn't shoot the messenger. We asked the Duchenes to investigate this on our behalf and so we cannot brush aside their findings because we don't like the implications. None of us are completely naïve. We know that there's a cost in revolution and that the party has its enemies. Are we not sending men and women to Spain to kill fascists? Comrade Vincent was held in high esteem, but we need to consider that he may have been defecting to the Trotskyists.'

Bigarde, on the opposite side of the table, pointed a finger at Bloyer. 'Are you suggesting he was a traitor to the party?'

'It saddens me to say this, but yes. He wouldn't have seen it that way, of course. No one sees themselves as a traitor. Instead they feel that they're doing the right thing for the greater good. Clearly, he was misguided and had compromised his ideals.'

'I just want to be clear,' Duchene said. 'This is not what I'm saying happened.'

Bloyer smiled and winked. 'Yes, we understand and thank you, Monsieur, for your discretion, which is appreciated. Comrade Duchene, could you please summarise the situation for us?'

Sabine blinked as all eyes in the room turned to her.

'Me?'

'Yes, please,' Bigarde said. 'As the party investigator, could you summarise?'

Sabine presented the key points. How Marcus Vincent, probably carrying the International Brigade money, had met Aaron Meunier at Le Drapeau. How, later that evening, Vincent had been killed and then Meunier murdered in his room.

'The fact that Meunier had come from Norway could suggest he was carrying a message or information either directly from Trotsky or via his supporters,' she said. 'Comrade Vincent and Meunier may have both been the victims of a killer or killers from or on behalf of Moscow. Meunier's passport confirms he was in Oslo.'

Bigarde looked up from the table. 'His passport?'

'Here.' Duchene slid the bloodied document across the table.

Bloyer peeled open the pages. 'They are correct, comrades, it was stamped in Oslo and then again in Le Havre.'

'Thank you, Comrade Duchene,' said Bigarde. 'Monsieur Duchene, anything to add?'

'No, I've said everything I wanted to.'

'Very good. Well, comrade, Monsieur, if you would be so kind as to wait outside while we discuss all this?'

Duchene paused at the door. 'You'll want to burn that when you're satisfied,' he said, pointing at the passport. 'I doubt the police will investigate Meunier's death if it's ever brought to their attention, but it would be best not to keep it lying around.'

~

'They're going to tell you we can stop investigating.'

Sabine nodded. 'I know.'

'They have the events in an order that makes sense to them, that explains what happened. You saw how Bloyer asked you to summarise, to legitimise it as coming from within the party. He knows how to manipulate a group.'

'I don't agree. He was trying to make sure I was recognised, by the party, for my work.'

'*Your* work?'

'Ours, *obviously*, but you don't want to be recognised by the French Communist Party.' A grin appeared at the corners of her mouth.

'No, indeed. Is Bloyer still going to Spain?' Duchene asked.

'I don't know. He was. Like you, he fought in the Great War. Now that he's acting as a member of the Central Committee, he might not. Why?'

'He likes you.'

'Auguste. Don't be jealous. We're comrades, nothing more.'

'He nominated you for that role.'

'The one he ended up winning.'

'It was clever. To appear not to want the position, to show largesse by putting you forward and not nominating himself. To impress them. To impress you.'

'Are you saying I wouldn't have been a good member of the Central Committee?'

The door to the meeting room opened, and Bloyer poked his head out.

'Excuse me for interrupting. We've made a decision.'

'That was quick,' Duchene said.

'What can I say? Sabine was convincing.'

# PARIS
## Monday, 16 November 1936

# TWENTY

Weary Métro commuters sat in silence, resigned to the thought of another four days of work. The low cloud of cigarette smoke and the weak lights of the carriage forced the newspaper readers to hold their the pages close to their faces.

Duchene was different. He was looking forward to tomorrow. He had his favourite class with some of his favourite students. Officially, of course, he said he liked them all, but among the other teachers and with Sabine he was less politic. Fourth grade English. Their final year of elementary school, advanced enough to tackle more sophisticated grammar and, for the most part, sophisticated enough to engage in wordplay.

Duchene returned the knowing nod from another commuter, who tipped his cap with his own folded copy of this morning's *L'Humanité* as Duchene opened his to page three. There was an article on Hugo Bloyer's election as acting member of the Central Committee, including a photo and a quote saying that he humbly accepted the nomination. Below this was a short obituary for Vincent.

## A.W. HAMMOND

### *Marcus Vincent – In Memoriam*
*14 May 1887 – 11 November 1936*

*It is with much sadness that we mark the passing of Comrade Marcus Vincent, a dedicated communist, unionist, leader and champion for all French workers, who died on 11 November after being attacked by persons unknown. As a merchant marine he joined the National Federation of Maritime Unions in 1903 and the French Communist Party in 1904. He served during the Great War and at its conclusion was voted a union delegate. At the Eighth Congress he was elected to the Central Committee for the PCF. Here, he formed part of the negotiating committee that worked with the French Section of the Workers' International to form the Popular Front and campaigned throughout the election on behalf of its nominees for the 1936 general election. He will be remembered by unionists and communists for his sacrifice and dedication to their cause. He is survived by his wife, Nora, and his two sons, Bertrand and Yves.*

No mention of fascists. No contradiction of the police. This satisfied Duchene. The explicit choice of words would avert street violence and, more importantly, any threat to his family.

And yet something about Vincent's story didn't sit well with Duchene. There was nothing unusual about him, nothing to suggest he would betray his party. Vincent had been unremarkable, and unremarkable men rarely challenge their own institutions. He had remained part of his union, fought when called on to do so, followed his party to its congresses and converted his experience of leading men at sea to leading them in their working life. There had been no reason for him to throw all this away.

Duchene went back through it all in his mind. From the party meeting to the boarding house to the encounter with Montfort in the cemetery, all the way back to the restaurant. There was something he was missing.

※

Marienne was at the table in the living room, reading her Agatha Christie.

He dropped his keys on the tray beside the door. 'Still good?'

'Shhh,' she said, without looking up.

'Sorry.'

Duchene hung up his coat and placed his satchel by the front door. He could hear Sabine in the kitchen.

He kissed her on the cheek. 'Good evening, my love.'

She was grilling slices of baguette while a potato and leek soup bubbled gently.

'You saw the paper.'

'The central committee kept their word.'

'You would have expected otherwise?'

'No. But it was reassuring to read it. Though I thought they'd embellished a little by referring to his "sacrifice" to the party.'

Sabine was staring at the soup as though it had some hidden meaning.

'How was your day?' he asked

'Lacking excitement.'

'Explain?'

She turned from the stove. 'The investigation. That was exciting. You and me, out on the street, seeking the truth, seeing through deception.'

'Outmanoeuvring landladies,' he said, pulling her towards him.

She pouted as she frowned but did not push him away. 'Yes. Even that old goat. And I'm not sorry to admit that finding that poor man's body was also thrilling. Putting the pieces together, connecting him to Trotsky. Is that what it's always like?'

'I have no idea. I've only done this once before. And that time I was mostly in the library reading newspaper articles. Sometimes you have to go backwards to go forwards.'

'Or unpick the knot… You have a lot of those sayings.'

'Maybe it's Marienne's influence. Those books she reads.'

'Or start at the beginning. You like that one the most.'

Duchene released her.

'What is it?'

'Save me some food. I'll be back soon.'

※

From the outside, Le Drapeau looked almost as if it was closed. To suit its name, a quilt of flags hung in the window, all French, with the tricolour looming largest in the centre. Around this were stitched relics from the past: a flag with four snakes around a white cross, a Huguenot battle flag, the revolutionary banner from the Paris Commune and something that appeared almost German with a black eagle, most likely at one time from Alsace. Also in the stitched collage of colour and shape was a replica of a medieval battle standard with a burning sun and, of course, the Bourbon flag with its three gold fleurs-de-lis on a blue background. The heavy, black drapes behind the quilts blocked out almost all the light from inside the brasserie. Only a small window above its door shed a pale glow over the restaurant's name on its lintel.

It was busy for a Monday, with all the booths and tables occupied. Duchene kept his coat on as the same waiter who had served him and Sabine approached.

'If you're on your own, I could seat you at the bar,' the man said as he smoothed down the tips of his waistcoat. There was the smell of alcohol on his breath.

'It's just you tonight?' Duchene asked. 'The last time I was here I had an excellent conversation with your bartender. I was hoping he might be here tonight.'

'I'm afraid it's just me.'

'Well, we'll have to see what we can manage, you and I.'

The waiter smirked and flapped his towel theatrically over the barstool. 'Sit, please, Monsieur.'

Duchene sat, then placed ten francs on the counter. 'Perhaps I could get us both a little something, something you think would go well with a cigarette.' He took out his Gauloises and offered one to the waiter, who checked the swing door to the kitchen before taking the cigarette.

The waiter poured Duchene a glass of wine, then filled a large teacup under the bar.

Duchene raised his glass. It was surprisingly good, worth much more than he'd paid. On seeing his reaction, the waiter winked and took a sip of his own drink.

'I was in here the other night,' Duchene said.

'So you said.'

'No, on Saturday. Do you remember?'

The waiter frowned. 'You were asking about the Trotskyist.'

'I was asking about a communist, this man, Marcus Vincent.' He produced the photo again.

'That's him. He was talking about Trotsky. With a man, from …Marseille. Wore a red scarf, his hair was still dark but he had a grey beard. Wore horn-rimmed glasses…that were…'

'*Octagonal* is the word you're looking for.'

'Yes, as I told you.'

'And who told you to tell me that?'

'I beg your pardon?'

'You provided almost exactly the same information as last time. Nothing extra, no new memory or recollection.'

'I'm not sure what you're suggesting?'

'I'm suggesting you're lying to me.' Duchene took a sip. The waiter stared at him, his jaw clenched tight. 'Here's the thing,' Duchene continued, 'the man you're describing is dead. The man you said he met is also dead. It makes you wonder if there are people who might like to guarantee your silence too, so that the lie you're telling never comes out. The faster you tell me the truth, the sooner we can make sure the killer is caught.'

The stiffness fell from the waiter's body, his shoulders dropped and he placed both hands on the counter. 'I don't know his name, the man who paid me to say those things, to give you that description.'

'Why?'

'Because he was the one who met this man, the one who ate here last week.' The waiter pointed to the photo of Vincent.

'He wanted me to tell anyone who asked that the man with the octagonal glasses was there instead. And that they were talking about Trotsky. He paid me an extra ten francs to say that, to remember it.'

'Here –' The waiter pulled a card out of his trouser pocket and put it beside the photo. They were the same size. On it was written the description of Aaron Meunier along with the phrase 'Talking about Trotsky'.

It took Duchene a moment to realise that the words were written on the back of a photo. He turned it over. It was the same official portrait of Marcus Vincent.

'The man who told you to say those words, he gave you this photo?'

'Yes.'

Duchene reached into his coat, took out his copy of L'*Humanité* and pointed at the photo of Hugo Bloyer.

'Was this the man?'

※

The veil of cloud that had descended on Paris, concealing the tops of apartments and steeples, was like a ceiling over the earth, bringing everything in close and causing Parisiennes to talk in muted voices as they moved through the streets. The air was crisp and still and smelt of woodsmoke. Duchene stood below a streetlight, watching the tall double doors of an apartment building opposite. They would once have been used for carriages and goods carts, which would have passed through a wide archway beyond that led into a small courtyard surrounded by apartments. Here the residents would have raised garden beds of herbs and vegetables, with children's fairy gardens dotted among them. The cats that lived in the building would be known by all and neighbours would occasionally hold window to window conversations across the courtyard. He envied this lifestyle, the way it harked back to an older, smaller Paris where community was valued. Now that the city had grown, anonymity and isolation were more common. He only knew one of his neighbours, Camille, and in truth she had sought out his family and made the effort to befriend them.

A figure dressed in a bulky coat, scarf and wide-brimmed hat stepped out of the apartment. He caught sight of Duchene under the streetlight and paused, not ready to close the door behind him just yet.

'Duchene?' Bloyer called.

'Yes.'

Bloyer locked the door and crossed the street towards him.

'It's a cold night. This couldn't wait until tomorrow?'

'I have classes to teach tomorrow.'

'Then maybe after that? Or in a break between classes? Your school must have a phone.'

'We have several.'

'It's an admirable profession, teaching. Especially languages, communication. You're bringing Europe closer together.'

'If it doesn't catch fire first.'

'Oh, please. You're sounding like your wife.'

'She's starting to bring me around to her way of thinking.' Duchene gestured down the street and they began to walk.

Bloyer, hands in his pockets, also assumed a casual tone. 'The

Spanish Republic and International Brigades will defeat the fascists and the Italians and Germans will retreat to their dens, their failure a demonstration to the people that their worldview is flawed. It might take a few more years, but they will lose favour and their people will see what can be achieved by collectivisation and organised industrialisation. They'll come to see the value of communism and we'll be there to guide them towards it.'

'Seems a bit optimistic,' said Duchene.

'Better to go to Spain with a grand vision – something more than just fighting the fascists. We need more from our future than merely an end to fascism.'

'So will you be going?'

'To Spain? No. No… I've reconsidered in light of recent events. I need to be here to support the Central Committee. I know Sabine will be disappointed, but I suspect she's already worked it out. Like you, I hung up my sword when the Great War ended.'

Duchene found himself rankling at the use of his wife's name. Men like Bloyer were convinced of their own significance in the lives of others. Except, perhaps, that in this case there was some truth to it, which made him dislike the man all the more.

Duchene guided them towards the river. 'I read Vincent's obituary today.'

'It was a disappointment, dry. But the committee didn't want to celebrate him too loudly in case his being a Trotskyist ever came out. That way they can distance themselves if necessary. I disagreed, but there you go. I wanted to recognise in more detail all that he'd done for the people and the party. Yes, he was a traitor in his final days, but we should pay tribute to all the days before that.'

The Seine lapped at its concrete banks. A lone barge moved slowly past, caught out late, risking a voyage on inky blackness.

'Except that he wasn't a traitor.'

Bloyer stopped and leant on the iron railing dividing the pavement from the lower boulevard that ran along the river's edge. His broad shoulders were relaxed, his arms spread just far enough to support him. He had the confidence of someone who knew their place in the city, and that place was nowhere near the bottom.

'I always knew there was a risk that you would discover the truth,' Bloyer said.

Duchene kept his eyes on the other man's hands.

'Sabine knows I'm meeting you. If anything –'

'Oh please, don't be so dramatic.' Bloyer was smiling as he turned his back to the river and took out a hip flask and a packet of Gauloises.

Duchene paused at the offer of a cigarette.

'Take one. It's polite. You're here to have a conversation, so let's have a proper one.'

Duchene lit his cigarette while Bloyer took a sip from the hip flask, before offering it to Duchene. 'Brandy?'

The hit of alcohol rushed through Duchene, sharpened his mind.

'So what have you discovered?' asked Bloyer.

'You made it appear that Vincent was a Trotskyist.'

'You've already alluded to that. What else?'

'You took the money and hid it in Meunier's room to make it appear that Vincent had stolen it and was giving it to the Trotskyists.'

'How do you imagine I did that? It was in a safe and I didn't have the key until after it went missing.'

'Because it was never actually in the safe. Sabine said you and some of the steelworkers had escorted her through the city to make sure she wasn't robbed. She said that you carried the money for her. I'm guessing that's when you swapped it. If I were to go back to her, and ask her to recall the events exactly, she would tell me you gave Vincent the money. I'm sure there was something clever with envelopes, something to disguise the fake money as something that Vincent might have legitimately placed in the safe. A fake bank cheque perhaps, something he wouldn't think to differentiate, something Langlois wouldn't look for when searching for the cash.'

Bloyer took another swig of brandy. 'That's very close. Well done.'

For some reason Bloyer was taking satisfaction in the revelations. There was delight in his eyes and he smiled at each new connection Duchene was able to demonstrate. And then it struck him.

'You approached Sabine to ask me to investigate. You needed someone to follow the breadcrumbs you'd left so that they pointed to Vincent, present the evidence that connected him to a dead Trotskyist. You even stage-managed the room in the boarding house. It never made sense that the killer would enter and exit through the window but leave the door open. That open window was all theatre, to support the story of a Moscow assassin. You left the door unlocked so we could easily discover the body. What I don't understand was why you wished to make it appear that Vincent was going to betray the party.'

'I would have thought that much was obvious. To discredit him, to implicate his murder in Trotskyism, to keep the party from looking too closely for fear of upsetting Moscow. By drawing attention to Stalin's leadership purges, those foundations on which Russian communism is built, the Central Committee would quickly look away. It was ugly, but it was necessary.'

'It was opportunism,' said Duchene. 'You killed Vincent to take his position, unelected, by using your influence with the committee.'

Bloyer shrugged. 'He lacked the sophistication to guide the party in the right direction. He would have had the unions blocking production in the factories, shutting down the Métro, because he didn't agree with our joining the Popular Front and our work with the socialists. He didn't appreciate that we needed to bring over the socialists, and bring all of France into a Soviet republic. He couldn't see the big picture and how to realise the goals of the Third International.'

'You speak the rhetoric well, but you're not a believer. You're just a murderer willing to do anything to put himself in power.'

'Believe what you will.'

Below them, vagrants in tattered clothes were gathering under a bridge. Clustered in a rough circle, they were sharing a bottle of wine, cigarette butts and a baguette.

'So why kill Meunier? Was that as a favour to Moscow?'

'An exchange. They would support my goals if I supported theirs. Meunier did have a letter from Trotsky. The Paris Trotskyists were going to publish it and it would have received international attention. Which would contradict Stalin and everything the Soviet Central Committee has been saying about the trials and the Trotskyist threat to communism. Everything you pieced together from the boarding house, the passport, where he had been and why he was here, it was all true.'

'What happened to the letter?'

'It's on its way to Moscow. If Trotsky tries again to communicate with the world, Moscow will want to know what he's trying to say.'

'So Moscow requested you to kill Meunier?'

'They did. I knew the city, how to make sure the police wouldn't look too hard at his death, even how it could act as a reminder to the Central Committee itself – that a global revolution may require bloodshed but it's the boss who decides whose blood gets shed…'

'You did the same with Vincent, made sure the police would put the case aside quickly. You gave them the letters.'

'…and fed them the line that the murder might have been politically motivated.'

'It was. But by communists, not by fascists.'

Bloyer took another drag on his cigarette and smiled. There was a self-satisfaction about him, rugged up warmly with liquor in his coat pocket, ready for a long talk, happy to indulge Duchene's conclusions. He had come prepared and now Duchene understood.

'You want an audience for your grand plan, someone to see the full picture and acknowledge your genius.'

'If you must give the compliment, then I will accept it.'

'You're very confident for someone who's admitted to murdering two men.'

'And you will do what with this information? Take it to the police, embarrass them by contradicting their finding? And your evidence is, what? The word of a waiter in a restaurant that hosts political agitators and revolutionaries? He's hardly a trustworthy witness. Perhaps you'll send them to talk to Montfort who, as we already know, is deeply suspicious. I'm confident because I know I can get away with it.'

'I'll tell the party.'

'And have them remove me? At the cost of exposing Stalin? I think not. It will be regrettable, and I'll lose some trust with them, but I can recover. They are, after all, just the Central Committee, and it's the party members who ultimately vote to install their leadership. No, you can try that, but it will only set me back a little.'

'I'll tell Sabine.'

The smile disappeared from Bloyer's face. He stubbed his cigarette out on the railing.

'That would be a shame. I like your wife. I consider her a friend. I wouldn't like her disappointment. But even that I'd survive. She'll be away in Spain. I'll be here in Paris. Our lives will move on and I'll learn to live with the loss.' He flicked the butt into the Seine. 'So yes, Monsieur Duchene, you have found a way to hurt me. Congratulations. But I'd ask you this: If you were to tell her, all of this, how it's actually connected, the Stalinist-sponsored assassination, the way in which I arranged my election, how the PCF would be trapped even if they knew what really happened… If you were to tell her all of this…truth…what would she think of you then?'

## TWENTY-ONE

Duchene couldn't go home. He couldn't. He needed to think, to plan. Anger kept swelling up within him, swamping his logic, dragging down his clear thinking. He wanted to wipe that lizard smile from Bloyer's face. Have him dragged before the workers he claimed to represent and revealed as a murderer, a manipulator and a fraud. Put an end to his political aspirations, hold him to account for his actions.

Perhaps Sabine could communicate it to the General Confederation of Labour, who could share it with other union leaders? There was a way to bring this to light, if not via the PCF leadership, then through the collectives that made up its membership. She needed to understand that the party she was part of, that was sending men and women off to fight and die, was itself an instrument of murder and deception. Where it was too easy to push this aside when it came to Stalin and Russia, it would be hard for her to ignore her own party's culpability.

This could be the thing, the perfect thing, that would stop her from going to Spain. It had nothing to do with him, or Marienne, or his desire that she stay safe in Paris. These were events beyond his control and they were the truth. Even better, she had come to him and asked him to find out who had killed Vincent. He had discovered the truth and she couldn't be angry with him for revealing it to her.

But as he stormed past the dual towers and carved façade of L'Eglise Saint-Ambroise, he remembered their bringing Marienne here to play when she had just started walking. Under the rose window, tottering on unstable feet, she had tried to snatch daisies from the church lawns. With the endearing awkwardness of a small child, she couldn't break the stems and had pulled up a handful of petals, which he helped her to throw into the wind. He felt his confidence waver.

The truth would hurt Sabine. It would change so much of her world. And yet, surely that was the point? She would be insulted if he kept it from her. She would feel patronised.

He shouted into the air.

And walked home.

---

Sabine was on the couch with Marienne curled up against her. They were listening to an amateur singing competition on the radio. An announcer was explaining that performers who failed to satisfy the judges would be pulled from the stage with a hook. The current singer was also playing the accordion badly, and mother and daughter laughed when the announcer described the hook nearing him. Marienne placed her hands over her face as the studio audience cheered when the man was removed.

Sabine smiled up at Duchene. 'Did you do what you needed to?'

'Just one last thought. Just one last thing.'

'And?'

'Can we talk?'

Sabine nodded and took her coat from its hook as Marienne repositioned herself, still transfixed by the radio.

'Back soon,' he told her.

He and Sabine stepped outside onto the fire escape, climbing through a window that Duchene chocked open with a small block of wood he kept on the sill. Sabine's movements were smooth and assured as she climbed ahead of him up the metal stairs to the building's roof.

From here they could see the rooftops of the city, sharp angles of zinc and stone peppered with stout chimney pots. Below these the lights from apartments glowed. A light wind had parted the clouds to reveal glimpses of the stars.

'It's a beautiful night,' he said.

'It is,' she replied, 'but we've seen better views from up here. It is Paris after all.'

'Vincent's obituary said he moved from the country to Paris. Like you.'

'It's a common story. Why are we here?' she asked, pulling up a crate.

'Would you want to know everything, if I learnt more about Vincent's death?'

'Yes.'

'And if it meant we keep going, even though the PCF have concluded the investigation?'

'Absolutely. I want to know the truth. Is this hypothetical or have you actually uncovered something?'

He pulled up a crate beside her and placed his hands around hers. Sabine's cheeks and the tip of her nose were turning pink in the cold night air. Her blue eyes gazed at him steadily. He wanted to stay here, looking into them, to hold her warmth, to hold this moment. Perhaps that's all it was, selfishness. To say any more about Bloyer and the murder would take this version of her away from him.

And so he chose not to.

'I went to the Seine. To Pont Royal and Pont du Carrousel.'

'Why?'

'Vagrants sleep under the bridges. I asked them if they had seen who'd put Vincent's body in the river. I didn't find anything. It was a bit of a gamble. It would take nights to interview them all, and more cigarettes than I could afford to pay them for their time.'

Sabine pulled her hands out of his. 'That's it? I thought you were going to tell me something, I don't know, earth shattering.'

'No.'

'Then why are we up here?'

'I want to talk to you about Spain. Properly.'

'I'm going. We've already discussed it.'

He felt the anger swelling up again, but took a deep breath and managed to push it back down.

'I know. I wanted to tell you I understand why you want to go, why you need to go.'

'You do?'

'I do.'

Sabine spoke in a low voice. 'I've seen photos of dead children, placed in rows to show the aftermath of a fascist air raid. You would think they were sleeping, if it wasn't for the blood smeared across them. They did this to make people understand the tragedy. Can you imagine holding the corpse of your own child, what that would be like?'

She still held his gaze. There were tears in her eyes. He dabbed at them with the corner of his sleeve.

'I cannot. I hope I never will.'

'That's why I'm doing this. For us. For Marienne. I want her to see that these people and their ideas need to be fought against. That we can't stand by and let them burn the world down around us.'

She looked up at Duchene.

'I don't want to leave her. I wish I could take you both with me. Or that there was some other way to fight the way the world is changing, without having to leave Paris. I know you've told me to stay, and part of me feels that I should, as a mother, but I worry about what I will become if I don't do this. The questions I will ask myself, the anger and disgust I'll feel. What kind of mother would I be then?'

Duchene put an arm around her shoulder. She pressed into him and sighed.

'We will need to explain it to her,' he said. 'Need to tell her about the war, the fascists, why you're going to fight. She's growing up fast, she understands much more than I did when I was her age.'

'But not tonight.'

'No. Not tonight. But soon.'

'I leave in two weeks.'

'Then let us find a way to make them two weeks to cherish.'

# BERLIN
## Saturday, 4 August 1945

## TWENTY-TWO

A gramophone was playing mid-tempo jazz. Something to keep the conversation lively and flowing, but not so frantic as to draw attention away from the celebrations and meetings taking place in the hotel bar. Raye was staring into his bourbon.

'Why do you do it?' Duchene asked. 'The card reading?'

'What's that?' Raye stirred and looked over at Duchene from his quilted armchair.

'You read the cards for soldiers. Why?'

'Helps with morale.'

'Because you only give them good news?'

'I give them realistic news, just enough hope to make their time here seem worth it. I started it when we were in the Ardennes. They...I...needed the distraction. When we weren't on the front line, when we were able to get some rest, there'd be a queue.'

'If it's only ever good news, you're not actually reading the cards.'

Raye returned his gaze to the bourbon. Duchene was drinking the same, in solidarity. Normally he found the liquor too sweet, but now that he was three measures in, it was growing on him.

'It's about interpretation, so who's to say if I'm doing it wrong.'

'Do you believe it?'

'I learnt it from my grandmother. And she believed. For some people it's truth. Who am I to say it isn't? Don't want to get a gris-gris on me – a curse.'

Raye was maudlin and this line of conversation wasn't going to pull him out of that. He realised this himself.

'They're gonna get it out of Allmann,' Raye said. 'Wring out everything that he knows, right down to the name of his hamster when he was a kid.'

'That's assuming he knows something useful.'

'Like you said, Sprenger called him a traitor for a reason. It might have been helpful to understand why.'

Raye finished his drink. 'Alright, I'm off to bed. In the morning, after breakfast, we'll head back to Andrews Barracks. Pack your bag and bring the tortoise. You'll be heading back to Paris on the next flight out of Tempelhof.'

Raye stood slowly and used the back of the chair to steady himself as he took a reading on which direction to walk in.

'Bonne nuit.' Raye tipped a finger to his forehead before swaying through the crowd and into the elevator.

Duchene picked up his glass from the walnut table and took a last sip. There was more bourbon, mostly in the bottle, but some splashes had made it to the polished surface. When they'd started drinking, surrounded by men in dress uniforms and women in silk and satin, Duchene had been uncomfortable with the opulence, after everything he'd seen out there in Berlin. The differences, he thought, in the way occupiers and the occupied lived. He'd seen it in Paris with the Germans; here it was reversed, the French, the British and the Americans. Why was he excluding the Soviets?

Perhaps he assumed that their dour officers wouldn't be afforded such luxury and excess. As he'd drunk more, though, he'd found himself less concerned by matters of politics and excess and started to enjoy the evening for what it was, a rare moment to celebrate that he was alive, that he had somehow survived his second war.

Duchene picked up the bottle and poured himself another shot.

'Care to pour one of those for me?'

He looked up to see Sabine standing beside him.

She wore a sleeveless blue pencil dress and her hair was caught up in a chignon. There were fine lines etched at the edges of her mouth and between her sculpted brows, a subtle notation of the years that had passed.

'I'll take it as a compliment that you're staring.' She smoothed the dress over her hips as she sat down.

He looked around the room, unsure if this it was an elaborate trap.

Sabine laughed. 'It's just me.'

Duchene tried to force his mind into focus. The liquor was blurring everything, not just his vision. He needed time to puzzle out why she had arrived here, at this moment.

'You look as though you just stepped here from Paris,' he said.

'In a way of speaking, I did. It just took eight years,' she smiled.

'If they find you here, they'll arrest you.'

Sabine laughed. 'Excusez-moi,' she said, gesturing to a black-jacketed waiter before switching to her heavily accented English. 'May I have another glass?' She held up Raye's used tumbler.

'Of course, Madame.'

'Merci.' She returned her gaze to Duchene. 'They think I'm French, because I *am* French. If I was dressed in one of those potato sack uniforms and speaking Russian they would arrest me. But as long as you keep this a secret, we will be fine.'

'You took Allmann.'

'We exchanged him. For some Americans.'

'You couldn't have been sure they'd make the deal.'

'No. But you didn't give us much choice after you shot Sprenger. It was a risk worth taking.'

'Sprenger shot Sprenger.'

'Huh. Interesting. I requested something we could use to exchange for the Gestapo – we've made prisoner swaps before. I was told we had some Americans, well looked after by the Red Army since we liberated them from a work camp. They were lucky we found them alive. Do you know what an SS officer said to me when we questioned him after we took Berlin? When we asked him why some of his prisoners were still alive? He said, "We spared those ones as proof we killed no prisoners." He was serious, couldn't see the irony in it. But perhaps there is no irony left in Europe? All forgotten as soon as we learnt of their death squads and concentration camps.'

Sabine tipped the waiter an American dollar when he returned with a fresh glass.

'You've come prepared,' Duchene said as he poured her a drink.

Sabine opened her arms in a model pose. 'I hoped you'd like it. I get few chances to dress up.'

He stiffened as he tried to maintain composure. Anger and desire were welling within him – so many years and not a word, so many years and his attraction for her hadn't waned.

'Not entirely the response I was looking for.' She held out her glass. As they toasted, she said, 'Za zdaróvye.'

Duchene frowned and Sabine laughed. 'So serious. Some things have not changed.' She crossed her legs, bouncing a black pump on the lip of the table. 'Come on, Auguste, I could do with a break from giving orders to farm boys and negotiating with career generals.'

On her left hand was her wedding ring, a signal she would have known he would notice.

'Alright, I'll bite. What happened? After you left Spain?'

'As you know, it didn't go well for us.' She reached down and took out one of Duchene's cigarettes. He lit it for her.

'You've picked up the habit.'

'After you've been shot twice, smoking feels like a triumph over the future.' She spoke quickly now, her eyes on the table, as she plotted her way through words she must have prepared earlier that evening. 'When the Soviets reassigned my commander, I retreated to Russia. I was going to come home, I wanted to come home, but then the war broke out. France was invaded and I didn't want to bring the danger of my being a communist to our house. So, I campaigned for the Soviets to enter the war against the Nazis. I had access to some generals who were sympathetic, but it took the Germans invading Russia for them to tear up the pact. And that's how I ended up in the Red Army, fighting fascists to liberate Europe.'

A calm had descended now, and she looked up at him.

'Major Sabina Dubovoya. That's what they call me. It's the closest thing to a Russian version of our surname.'

She was watching for his reaction. He did his best not to give her one.

'Major,' he said, 'that's quite the rank.'

'Thank you,' she said, taking a sip of the bourbon before returning her glass to its coaster. 'They won't even let women serve in combat roles in France.'

'Not in the French army, not normally. They did let women fight in the French Forces of the Interior. That's where Marienne ended up, fighting in the liberation of Paris and France. Now she's on assignment for a newspaper in Algeria.'

Sabine's poise and composure were suddenly gone. Her shoulders dropped and she covered her face with her hands.

'Thank God.' She took a napkin from the table and dabbed at her eyes. 'I didn't want to ask. I didn't feel I had any right to.'

He didn't realise it had happened. One moment he was sitting back in the armchair, trying to read her calculated movements and interpret their meaning – seek out the deception, uncover the trap; the next he had his hand on hers, comforting her.

'She's your daughter, of course you have a right.'

'I just couldn't write to you. It seemed cruel, to tell you I was returning to war, to maybe die, almost die, just survive. What was I to say, "Don't write back, I need to know that you are frozen in a moment, safe in 1936"? I had to close myself off from that part of me that was a mother and a wife.'

'You still have your ring.'

'Of course.'

'So you're still my wife?'

'I will always be your wife.' She took a deep breath, then kissed his hand and released it. She dragged on her Lucky Strike. 'It also helps with the way the Soviets regard me. To them I am just a soldier and not a potential conquest. So tell me, how is Marienne now that she is a woman?'

'She's become more and more like you. People are drawn towards her, they want to be in her presence, and listen when she speaks. She's smart, is clever with wordplay, still reads, speaks German and English as well as I do. Still has a strong will and knows her own mind…'

'Makes your life hell.'

Duchene laughed. 'Makes my life hell. But she makes it so worthwhile in every other way. I couldn't be prouder of what she's become. Here.'

He reached into his pocket and took out the photo and the letter from Sétif. 'This came from her last week.'

Sabine freed her hands of distraction so she could grasp the photo and stare into it, her eyes tracing the image, a smile growing on her face. Mother and daughter shared the same dark hair and broad smile, but that was where the close resemblance ceased.

'She doesn't look much like me.'

'Nor me. She's her own self. She's constantly trying to make sure I'm safe. I don't think she'd approve that I'm here. But then, I probably wouldn't have encouraged her to go to Algeria. There's also this.'

He passed the letter to Sabine. Her expression was animated as she read.

'She says there's been a massacre?'

'That's what it looks like – Algerians killed by our own army.'

Sabine shook her head as she returned the letter and the photo. 'Is this what we fight for?'

'I never thought so. But she's going to investigate, going to report on it.'

'Like father, like daughter.'

'Like mother too, it would seem.'

Sabine finished her drink and Duchene poured her another.

'What can I say?' She lit a second cigarette off her first. 'I never forgot what it was like in Paris, when we investigated Marcus Vincent's murder. Do you still remember it?'

'I do.'

'It made quite the impression on me. I still use some of your techniques. I have others of my own now.'

'My techniques?'

'Go back to the beginning – that's how we found Allmann. The Red Army had captured a few of the Oberführer's men, who gave up his name and those of his trusted lieutenants. Allmann was one. So when I heard the Americans were keeping a group of Gestapo in an old POW camp, I got them to rush the request. I was expecting to arrive and find you'd already pulled him out of the group. It was a gamble.'

'How did you find out about the camp?'

'We're all in the same city, Auguste. The information flows. You'll have your own informants just like we have ours.'

'I don't have any informants.'

'Really? I'd assumed they'd reinstated you.'

'No. I refused.'

'Hmm. So it's Citizen Duchene, then?'

'How long have you been working for Soviet intelligence?'

'I was assigned to the Main Intelligence Directorate when they knew I spoke French and German. A useful pair of languages. Then I trained at the Lenin Military-Political Academy. I've completed sixteen assignments. This is number seventeen.'

'Are you sure you should be sharing this all with me?'

Sabine stopped smiling and held his gaze. 'If an NKVD agent were to be sitting in this bar right now, they'd be unlikely to speak French and, even so, they wouldn't be close enough to hear us. Besides, I'm here working on an investigation that happens to include my husband, from whom I'm extracting information.'

'I'm not sure if the USSR is all that interested in the activities of our daughter.'

'And I hope they never will be.'

He topped up his drink and did the same for Sabine.

'You're wise to be cautious about them,' Duchene said.

'And you'd be wise to be cautious about the French government, and the Americans.'

The tip of her cigarette glowed and faded and glowed again.

Duchene sat forward in his chair. 'I never told you at the time but Bloyer murdered Vincent and –'

'– Meunier. I know.'

'How?'

'I wasn't completely naïve. You came back that night, told me you'd be talking to vagrants. It didn't make sense. So I went back to the beginning, back to the money that was stolen. That was the first movement.'

'Movement?'

'Like a symphony. I think of an investigation like music.'

'For me it's chess.'

'I thought it was a ball of wool?' She laughed. 'The first "crime" committed was the theft. Bloyer had held the money for me, given it to Vincent. It made me suspicious, about how it had been placed in that room, almost as though we were meant to find it.'

'Clever. And it didn't change your perception of the party?'

'Of course it did, but I moved on. Do you know what happened to Bloyer?'

'I tried to keep track of him but things became difficult in the war. He was formally voted onto the Central Committee in '37. The PCF did arm itself and fought as part of the resistance. But as for specifics, I don't know. He hasn't re-emerged since the occupation.'

'He didn't join de Gaulle's government?'

'He may not have survived. He may have been sent to a camp, he may have been executed, he may have fled to the country… a lot happened. It hardly seems the point anymore, to bring him to justice.'

'No,' she said, 'it does not.'

Sabine moved closer to him. He could smell the bourbon on her breath. The violet hour, the last of the day's light, had arrived, framed by arched windows. It felt to Duchene that he and Sabine were in their own private world.

'Why didn't you say anything? On the rooftop?'

'I wanted to. I was going to. But I also thought it might seem as though I was trying to make you distrust the party.'

'Because if they knew the truth about Bloyer, they wouldn't act against him? Because he killed that Trotskyist on orders from Moscow?'

'Yes,' Duchene replied. 'And because your ideology was so clear and righteous and it seemed wrong to do anything that might undermine it. And, selfishly, I didn't want you to think I was getting any satisfaction from showing how complicit they all were. You were so determined to go to Spain and we had such a short time together before you left, I didn't want to ruin any of that. Why didn't you tell me you'd worked it out?'

'I wasn't sure. It was just a theory. Then I sensed that Bloyer was behaving differently towards me, becoming more distant. I was angry, but I eventually I thought, you know, what is to be gained by confronting you with a deception, because I realised soon enough that you thought you were doing the right thing, to protect me. And though I don't need you to protect me, I appreciated the gesture.'

She reached out and touched the plaster on Duchene's head. Her hands were warm, her fingers moved lightly across his skin. 'It would seem I'm not the one who needs protecting.'

'I was stupid – fell over.'

'Fell over into someone's rifle butt.'

'It's nothing.'

'I could have him shot,' she smiled.

He paused and moved his head slightly, away from hers.

'Joking,' she said and kissed his lips.

She was tentative and cautious. With one hand on her arm, the other cradling her head, he pulled her closer. Their bodies met between the two chairs and now she was gripping him harder, breathing him in. Beneath the unfamiliar floral perfume she now wore, there came to Duchene a scent-memory – of sea and clay – and he knew it was truly her, the Sabine he had always loved.

She released him, kissed him again and moved back into her chair. Her cheeks were flushed and he could feel the warmth in his own face.

'Well, that was something,' she said. 'I wanted to do that the moment I arrived.'

'I'm glad that you did.'

'We should do it some more. You have a room?'

He nodded and reached out his hand.

Sabine picked up the bottle from the table and led him through the bar and towards the elevator.

'Room one zero six,' he said, pulling the key from his pocket.

The elevator opened and she punched in the floor, pulling him towards her by his lapels as the doors closed and they rose towards the first floor. She kissed him harder this time, biting his neck.

Soon he was scrabbling at the lock and they were in the room, simple but well appointed with its wood-panelled walls. Sabine released him onto the bed, then poured them another drink at the small bar table. She slipped her shoes off and padded barefoot towards him, a glass in each hand.

A rustling sound came from the basket on the floor.

Sabine raised an eyebrow. 'I wasn't going to ask, but now I have to. What's that?'

'A basket.'

'Funny. What's in it?'

'A tortoise.'

'Yours? Or spoils of war?'

'Mine. Yes.'

She passed him both drinks and hitched her dress up to her hips. She straddled him, took her glass back and swallowed a large slug of the liquor.

She smiled at him, warm and generous. 'Why do you have a tortoise in your room?'

'We really don't need to –'

She laughed. 'State secrets? Come on, now, tell me.'

'Just bad memories. I'm obligated to keep him alive. He's all that's left of the school.'

She moved slowly from his lap to sit beside him on the bed. 'What happened to the school?'

'We were bombed, during the occupation. They were aiming for a munitions factory but hit us instead. Somehow, Ernest survived. I've been looking after him ever since.'

Sabine pulled her dress back down over her knees and leant against Duchene.

'And all those children?'

Duchene shook his head. 'And you?'

'Fine. Except for the dreams.'

Sabine was staring at the basket.

'During the occupation – that's when they bombed you. So it was the Allies.'

Duchene nodded.

'Fuckers.'

'I don't blame them.'

'You should. They killed those children. Or are you saying they wouldn't have had to bomb the factories if the Germans hadn't been using them to make munitions?'

'That is true, but I don't think it's about a tally of wrongs and rights anymore. The Nazis were evil, what they did is unthinkable. But are we here to exact revenge on all Germans?'

Her voice was rising, shifting half an octave. 'You're saying they shouldn't be punished, that they should just be allowed to live their lives as though they hadn't killed millions of innocent people?'

'No. Not at all. I support the denazification of Germany, I agree there need to be reparations, I support Nuremberg. But I'm offended that the brutality goes on. We say we're more enlightened, but that's not entirely true. In France they're still hunting collaborators, without proof. They can't see how it prolongs the occupation, that we don't need the Gestapo to turn in our neighbours. We'll do it to ourselves. The witch-hunts and executions continue. You see the cycle? When do the Germans exact revenge on the Soviets for the children they killed during the destruction of Berlin, for the rape of their women?'

Sabine stood up. 'They don't get to.' She was breathing rapidly. 'None of that should ever have happened. If the Nazis had surrendered earlier, lives would have been saved. If our discipline had been better...it wasn't how it should have been. But *they* started this. You said it yourself, their ideology is evil.'

'I don't know if their civilians truly supported their crimes.'

'They didn't? I think you'll find that they supported them and fed and clothed the troops and cheered for the German war effort. They supported the ideology. They knew the Jews were going *somewhere*. They're only compliant now because they were decisively defeated. By us.'

'You're picking around your arguments – the Red Army's crimes are regrettable, but they're not accountable, but German civilians are?'

Sabine returned to the bar table and turned her back to him to pour more bourbon into her glass.

'I've seen things. You have no idea. Piles of dead, slaughtered in their concentration camps, mass graves of women still clutching their children in their arms. You would think I'd be used to it. I'm not. How does someone get used to that much murder? And what does it say about them if they do?'

Now standing beside her, he placed a hand on her shoulder. 'Do you sleep?'

'Do you?'

'Not well.'

She sighed. 'Why are we talking about this? You couldn't let this pass, just for an evening?'

'I didn't.'

'You judge me, what we're doing. The world isn't that simple.'

'I agree. But you're ignoring what's going on around you. Stalin is dangerous, his ideology is dangerous. He may not be a fascist, but he *is* a dictator.'

'You can't understand what we've been through, to bring socialism to the world, to seize power for the working classes, to finally build a classless society.'

'What's really going on? You can't honestly believe the rhetoric?'

'And you honestly believe, what, the rhetoric of capitalists? You're here in Berlin as their pawn, chasing down plans for rockets that will be used to threaten us with war. Or do you now believe that weapons are instruments of peace? You're a hypocrite.'

She was staring at him, her eyes burning with anger. Her feet were planted squarely, her body rigid, her hands curled into fists.

'We have nothing in common.' Her voice was without emotion. 'You don't understand me at all. I'm not sure you ever have.'

'I understood you enough to support you going to Spain.'

'I did that to make a difference –'

'For Marienne, yes, I know.'

'And I have. But you, you're a man broken by war, afraid to believe in a cause because doing so might threaten your safety. The world changes but you don't want to change with it. You haven't altered at all.'

'And I'm sorry that you have.'

Sabine's body relaxed, not into softness but something more like numbness. Her eyes went dull and she sighed again.

'So this is it.'

'It looks like it. Yes.'

'I had hoped this would be different.'

'So had I.'

Sabine took off the wedding ring and placed it on the bedside table, then spoke in a low voice. 'Don't follow me. Give up your search. I still want you to be safe.'

'I want you to be safe too.'

'Then let me do my job. Right now, you're the most dangerous thing to me. Each time you lead the Americans to me.'

There was a knock at the door.

Sabine looked across to Duchene, immediately alert, her eyes wide as she scanned the room. He could see her looking for something – a weapon, an exit. Her hand moved to the neck of the bourbon bottle.

The knock was repeated.

'Duchene.' It was Raye. 'Open up. We've got to talk.'

Sabine whispered, 'The American.'

Instantly, he could feel the question poised in the air, and from Sabine's expression he could see that she could too. Open the door to Raye, try to arrest her, stop the Russians. Better yet, he could stop her from returning to them. Make her see how wrong she was to continue to have faith in their cause.

Her hand tightened on the bottle. She would attack him? Just to flee.

'Auguste, get up. Come to the door. It's about your wife. We need to talk.'

Duchene froze. Could he know? Was Raye standing outside with military police? Had he and Sabine been seen in the bar together?

Sabine continued to watch him. He held a finger to his lips.

'Just a moment,' he called.

Sabine moved swiftly. She threw open Duchene's valise and dug around in it until she found his trench knife.

'Always this thing,' she said, maybe to herself, maybe to him.

She used it to puncture her dress, just below the hip, and followed the seam until she had slashed open one side. She dropped the knife, grabbed her shoes from the floor and was at the window.

The warm night air stirred the curtains. In seconds, she had dropped her shoes to the street below and was climbing out onto the ledge. In a single movement she had turned and was hanging from the sill as her toes searched for a foothold.

'Hold on.' Duchene leant out and gripped her wrists so she could hold his forearms. 'It's a long way, let me help.'

He felt the window frame digging into the bottom of his rib cage as she used his arms to climb a little lower. Then she was holding only his fingers, her whole weight pulling on his sockets until they felt as if they were going to crack.

'Goodbye, Auguste.' She landed on the ground with a slap,

startling a young GI who was smoking on the low wall that ran along the canal.

'On se voit bientôt, mon amour,' she called up to the window.

The GI grinned and gave a thumbs up to Duchene. Sabine already had her shoes on and was running down the street.

## TWENTY-THREE

'What took you so long?' Raye asked.

He was alone. There were no soldiers. No one primed for an arrest.

'I was dozing. Then I thought I'd just pour us each a bourbon,' Duchene said, holding a glass towards Raye.

Raye went across to the open window. 'Thought I heard someone talking in here.'

Duchene lit a cigarette, puffing on it so that the smell of burning tobacco would overwhelm any lingering whiff of her perfume.

'That was me.'

Raye took a sip of his drink. 'Higher voice than yours. Speaking French.'

'Still me. I was talking to the tortoise.'

'The tortoise.'

'Sure. Like the way you do with a baby. Parler bébé.'

'My mawmaw used to do the same thing with her Trigg hounds back in Lafayette.'

'You said you wanted to talk about my wife?'

Raye blinked and turned back to the room. 'Yeah, she's not

going to give up on this thing. She was motivated enough to bring uniformed officers into the French zone and risk capture. Says to me she's got some rat lines of her own. Says to me that she won't hesitate to do it again. If those plans are still out there, she's going to find them. She won't give up.'

'Agreed,' Duchene said.

'So neither should we.'

'You're not ready to give up after all.'

'That was the bourbon talking. Makes me maudlin.'

'So we should stop drinking then?'

Raye took one more sip. 'Agreed.'

Duchene took the tortoise out of the basket and placed him on the floor before returning from the bathroom with an ashtray full of water. They both watched as the creature poked a sour-looking face out of his shell and started to drink.

'I suppose you're going to want to know why I have him?' Duchene asked.

'Nope. A man's personal business is his own, especially in wartime,' Raye said.

'So what's your plan?'

'We talk it through.'

'Not much of a plan.'

'No.'

'Alright,' said Duchene. 'We don't have Allmann.'

'We don't have any Gestapo that I know of.'

'Can you look for some more? They're SS so they'll have tattoos.'

'We've already done all that,' Raye replied. 'Even pulled some who had obviously tried to disguise that they'd had tattoos – cut them out or shot themselves through the arm… Going back to the Rhein camps isn't really an option.'

'We could re-interview his daughter? We didn't ask her about the plans.'

'Feels unlikely, given her feelings about him. I can't see Sprenger telling her anything, let alone leaving them with her for safekeeping.'

'Okay. Let's go back to Allmann. You said he had papers with him.'

'Yes, but intelligence officers would have gone over his vehicle. Rocket plans, troop movements, the location of Nazi leadership, forged documents – those would have gotten their attention immediately.'

'But did you look at the papers? Perhaps there's something that only you would see.'

Raye shot out of his seat. 'Come on. Grab your stuff.'

'Where are we going?'

'Back to the airport.'

---

The night was cooler now. Duchene, in the back seat of the jeep, had the basket on his lap, his valise beside him. Austin was following a small flow of traffic south out of Kreuzberg. The city was dark, save for some major roadways, where power had been restored. These cut through the blackness like glowing arteries.

After the guards at the gatehouse had gone through the formal motions of recording Raye's ID and time of entry, the jeep pulled up outside the Tempelhof terminal building.

Raye was out and already heading up the stairs towards a line of glass doors as he called back, 'Stay with the –'

'– vehicle. Yes, sir.' Austin pulled out his well-thumbed copy of Edgar Allen Poe, holding it close to his face and using his torch to improve the poor light cast by the lamppost above them.

Duchene dug around in his bag and took out his copy of *The Sun Also Rises*.

'This is yours?'

'Yours now. If you want it.'

'You're sure?'

Duchene nodded. 'I've read it many times. I think it needs a new reader now.'

'Thank you.' The corporal took the book carefully in both hands and stared at the cover, with its ruby-lipped woman in a green dress.

'Duchene!' Raye shouted. 'Come on.'

Although the building's corridors were still lit, the ground-floor offices were dark. All but one. Raye made a beeline for it.

Inside a bespectacled sergeant and two army clerks were pasting teleprinter messages onto sheets of paper.

'You're Gibson, yes? I spoke to you on the phone,' said Raye. 'You've got my Kübelwagen.'

'That's correct, sir. Please follow me.'

They left the cavernous terminal and walked out onto a concrete airfield that still radiated captured heat from the day. The only movement between the hangars and cargo bays was that of soldiers armed with rifles slung over their shoulders patrolling the length of the kilometre-long building. Out near the runway, a truck was refuelling an American air force plane, filling the surrounding air with the smell of petrol. It was shorter but wider than the aircraft Duchene had arrived on but painted in the same tan and olive camouflage. The voices and laughter of its crew cut across the still night as they stood around the plane drinking out of metal canteen cups.

They followed Gibson through an entrance beside the huge hangar door. Pulling on a lever, the sergeant thunked the oversized pendant lights into life. Long grids painted on the floor ran the length of the hangar and within the assigned spaces sat large storage containers, or pallets with smaller stacks of archive boxes, or German vehicles, including trucks, cars, bikes.

'You're looking for aisle four, bay twenty-two,' Gibson said, referring to his clipboard.

'Fantastic.' Raye clapped him on the back.

'And sir, I do need you to return that bike with the sidecar. I'm fielding questions.'

'I appreciate that. I'll file the paperwork with you tomorrow.'

'Paperwork?' The sergeant looked over his glasses. 'Sir, I –'

'I'm afraid you're going to have to ask the French if you want it back.' Raye looked out into the hangar. 'Can you get one of the clerks to run over some coffee? We're a bit sauced.'

Duchene followed Raye to a dark grey open-topped car, about the same size as a jeep but with low bucket seats. The iron cross on one door had been punctured by bullet holes. In the back was a US army archive box, a long canvas bag and two rectangular metal cases, dented and scratched.

Raye pulled out the box. 'This is a long shot.'

'There could be something. Sprenger called him a traitor.'

'Twice. I remember.'

'So aside from giving us Sprenger's name, what was Allmann's other betrayal?'

'Fleeing?' asked Raye.

'That would be a "coward".'

'They're SS. Fleeing *is* considered a betrayal.'

The box contained typed forms, grouped into years. Duchene scanned them. 'They seem to be details of information taken during interviews with informants. See here.' Duchene held one of the stacks towards Raye as he placed the box on the ground.

'What about prisoners?'

Duchene flicked through more of the papers. 'Nothing I can see. You said Allmann wanted to trade this for his safety?'

'That's what I was told. Maybe he was thinking that the names of Nazi collaborators, those you might want to punish after a war, could be valuable for the Allies. People who'd worked with the Gestapo.'

'Some of these interviews took place in Paris. If these got into the hands of vigilantes there'd be more reprisals.'

Raye continued to rummage through the papers. 'You're right. No interrogations.'

Duchene reached for one of the rectangular cases. Its cover was held in place by two clasps on the side.

'German radio. Well, one of them is. The other's the receiver.' Raye stood up and passed over a paperclipped set of pages. 'Here.'

Duchene looked down. He was holding the transcript of the Oberführer's two interviews with him.

'You might want to keep those.'

'They could exonerate me?'

'Don't know about that. It just lists the information you

provided. Doesn't go into how freely you gave it. In fact, they're marked as an interview, not an interrogation, so that's not a good thing...'

'Thank you.' Duchene folded the pages and put them in his pocket.

'Just don't say anything to Gibson.'

They heard the clang of the hangar door being opened as a clerk carrying a tray slowly made his way towards them.

Raye examined the radio. 'It's dialled in on a frequency here.'

'Do you know what it is?

'Don't recognise it, but I'm not a signalman so that doesn't really mean much. I'll make a note.'

The clerk's tray held coffee, milk and sugar and a small biscuit tin.

'Thank you, corporal,' Raye said. 'What's in the tin? If it's K-rations I'll be putting this coffee over your head.'

'No sir, honey cookies. The cook made them yesterday.'

'Very nice.' Raye sent the clerk on his way and popped open the tin to find four cookies inside. He stashed three in his pocket and offered the last one to Duchene.

'Just the one?'

'You just got your hands on some state secrets. You're lucky you got anything else.'

As Duchene munched, he pulled open one of the car's rear doors and hauled out the canvas bag. It was heavy and slid onto the hangar floor with a metal crash loud enough to make the clerk glance back on his way to the door.

Raye put his coffee on the bonnet of the car and helped Duchene to unfasten the buckles and leather straps.

'This doesn't look like standard issue,' Raye said as they looked down into the bag.

Inside were a rock pick, a masonry chisel, a trowel and a small half-empty bag marked 'Zement'.

Raye lifted the pick and touched his finger to its pointed end. 'What was he doing?'

'Burying something,' Duchene replied.

'Why all this stuff? Why not just use a spade?'

'Because he was putting it in a wall.'

# BERLIN
## Sunday, 5 August 1945

## TWENTY-FOUR

'I need a signals officer and First Sergeant Davis and her team. Now!' Raye's voice punctuated the silence of the night as he shouted at a stocky duty officer standing in the doorway of the small office at Andrews Barracks he and Duchene had commandeered the day before. Then, like a lesser Prometheus, he flicked switches along the halls to bring light to darkness.

Duchene could hear the duty officer on the phone, calling the barracks as they ascended the stairs.

'And coffee! And breakfast,' Raye added.

'Breakfast?'

'It's zero three hundred, that's officially morning.'

It occurred to Duchene that in another life, in Paris, he'd be having a night cap, not breakfast. He watched as Raye began to rearrange the furniture, moving chairs and dragging in desks from adjoining rooms.

A bleary-eyed soldier arrived at their door, his face pink from exertion, a comb moving from his hand to his pocket. His hair was roughly parted, but otherwise neat. The effort was wasted on Raye who, with his stubble, unkempt hair and dusty civilian clothes, was far from a professional-looking soldier.

'Private...?'

'Henderson, sir.'

'We need you to look at this.' Raye handed him his notepad. 'This bandwidth, what is it?'

The stared at the numbers. 'It's not one we'd use.'

'We found it dialled into a German radio transmitter,' Duchene said. 'Most likely the date for the transmission would have been during the fall of Berlin.'

'Allmann was picked up on May first. So a day or two, maybe, before then,' Raye said.

The private nodded. 'Neither the Germans nor the Soviets would have used this frequency either.'

'Why? What is it?'

'Pretty sure it's a civilian frequency – the Germans would have used it for emergency broadcasts only. Anyone with a receiver, military or otherwise, could pick it up.'

'What was the range of a German transmitter? From an infantry man's backpack – field grey, three black dials?'

'That's a Torn.Fu.d2. The range depends on the setting for the output wattage.'

Raye rolled his eyes.

'We should have brought it with us,' Duchene said.

'That can still be arranged,' said Raye. 'What's the range between the highest and lowest setting?'

'Between four and ten kilometres, sir.'

Raye and Duchene moved to the map on the pinboard. 'That would include most of the city,' Duchene said.

More movement at the door – First Sergeant Davis and three other women. Again, Duchene was surprised by the speed with which they'd arrived, especially as they'd found the time to apply make-up and arrange their hair.

'First Sergeant Davis, we need the files we have on SS-Obersturmführer Allmann, starting with his movements.'

'If I may?' Duchene asked. Raye nodded. 'We also need any information on emergency radio transmissions from the twenty-eighth of April onwards.'

'Yes, sir, Monsieur Duchene.' Duchene could hear Davis in the hall, speaking calmly but directly as she gave her instructions.

Duchene turned to the signalman. 'And can you please find us a map of Germany? Something that shows us Berlin to the River Elbe.'

'Okay,' Raye said. 'We're thinking now that Allmann had the plans.'

'It's a leap,' Duchene said. 'We're looking for something that makes that a bit more certain.'

'So Allmann leaves Gestapo headquarters in Berlin carrying the names of informants to trade to the Allies, but along the way he stops to bury, sorry, hide something in a wall. We know this because he has tools and cement.'

'He also has a radio that he's used to transmit on the emergency frequency.'

Henderson returned with the map.

'Good job,' said Raye. 'Get it up on the board for us and start mapping out ten-kilometre points along the shortest distance from Berlin to where we had Allied forces on the Elbe.'

Duchene spoke again. 'We need to know what was in that broadcast.'

'Problem is, unless he was sending the signal just before he surrendered, we're not likely to have a record of it. Ten kilometres isn't far. We weren't even close to Berlin by then.'

'So, First Sergeant Davis is chasing a dead end?'

'Not necessarily. We don't know what we don't know.'

The signalman started marking out points along the map as Davis returned to the room.

'Allmann's file, sir. Not much in it, but it includes the statement he made when he was arrested and the formal interview.'

'Have you read it?'

'I did brief Major Greer the day before he flew out to Paris.'

Duchene took the file. 'When did Allmann leave Berlin?'

'The day after the RAF stopped bombing the city, Monsieur. He anticipated, correctly, that this meant the Soviets would be moving in. He could hear the shelling in the distance so he claimed that he left Berlin on May twenty-nine at zero seven thirty .'

'Signalman, can you mark that?'

Henderson made a note in red pencil on the map.

'He tried to cross at Torgau but the bridge was closed to everything but foot traffic. Somehow, he managed to get onto a barge and cross near Magdeburg, where the 102nd Division detained him on May thirty.'

'So if he came down from Berlin to Torgau, where would he go?' Raye asked.

'Ah, Ludwigsfelde…Luckenwalde and…Herzberg.' The signalman traced a line south from Berlin.

'And then from Torgau to Magdeburg?'

That would pass via Wittenberg…Wiesenberg…and Zerbst.' Henderson drew a line back up the map to follow the river. It made the shape of a U.

'Good. That's where we're looking for messages on the emergency frequencies. What's the time now?' Raye said, looking at his watch.

Duchene checked his. It was only 3.30 a.m.

'I'll need to give it another two hours at least. Alright,' Raye said to Davis and Henderson, 'you have your assignment. We're looking for anything picked up by Allied forces from those cities on the emergency broadcast between May twenty-nine and thirty. It's a long shot, but I need to know.'

'You're going to contact your informant,' Duchene said after others had left.

'Not my informant,' Raye replied. 'Not exactly. I'm owed a favour by the officer running them, and they have a line into the Soviets.'

'You want to know if the Russians received this emergency broadcast?'

'I do. They were on the outskirts of Berlin, within a ten-kilometre radius. They're more likely to have picked up something than us.'

'So what do we do between now and then?'

'Sleep.'

---

If he'd slept, if that's what you could even call it, he didn't dream. His mind was too alert to the sounds around him, the disciplined waking of the camp and quick resumption of daily tasks. His half-conscious mind kept turning to Sabine, falling into darkness and vanishing into the void.

*L'appel du vide...the call of the void.*

Was this what was dragging Sabine into yet more conflict? He had little knowledge of psychology, but had read that the passing idea to throw oneself off a tall building, perhaps, or a cliff, was not a desire to cease to exist. It was the opposite – the desire to live. Maybe this is what it was for Sabine, seeking out new dangerous ways to feed her appetite for life.

Someone knocked. Duchene opened his eyes to see First Sergeant Davis standing in the doorway. The grey light of the morning that framed her made him squint. He shielded his eyes with the back of his hand.

'Good morning.'

'Sorry to disturb you, Monsieur Duchene. Captain Raye has an update.'

Duchene heaved himself up from the couch. He felt stiffness and pain throughout his body. Worst of all was the headache behind his eyes.

'Would you like me to get you another one of those?' Davis was pointing to the uneaten breakfast still resting on its tray beside the couch.

'I'll be fine with it as it is. But coffee would be appreciated.'

'And aspirin?'

'Yes please. How did you –'

'Captain Raye asked for the same.'

Shoes and jacket on, Duchene slowly climbed the stairs to their commandeered office.

Raye was giving orders, but his eyes were fixed on a sheet of paper on the desk in front of him.

'You got your answer?' Duchene asked.

Raye looked up. 'An answer. I'm not sure how much it helps us. We've been staring at this for the last ten minutes and have come up with nothing.'

Davis arrived, followed by a steward bearing a tray with small rolls, sliced meats, a boiled egg and coffee. 'Traditional,' Duchene said. 'Thank you.'

'Just minus the beer,' Davis said. 'This is served to officers on a Sunday – to familiarise them with the German way of doing things.'

'Have a look at this,' Raye said.

He was staring at a short message written down in English: 'Werewolves rise up. Under victory lies our triumphant weapon. Heed the herald to war. Honour will always be our loyalty. Heil Hitler.'

'This message was broadcast four times on emergency channels from within Berlin on May twenty-nine. It's a coded resistance call.'

'It could be Allmann.'

'What makes you say that?' Raye asked.

'The reference to the werewolves. He spoke about them when we interviewed him at the POW camp. Who took down this message?'

'I did,' Raye replied.

'Did you translate it?'

'Already translated.'

'We need the original German,' said Duchene. 'This phrase, "under victory", doesn't really make sense. The rest reads like standard Nazi hot air, but that sticks out.'

'Hold on.' Raye raced out of the room.

Duchene sat down and started to tear open the bread, lay meat and cheese on it and sip at the coffee. He was almost finished when Raye returned.

'Here.' He thrust a new piece of paper at Duchene, who took it after wiping his fingers on a napkin.

The room fell silent as Duchene read the German aloud: 'Werwölfe erheben sich. Unter der Viktoria liegen die Waffen zu unserem Triumph. Ehre wird immer unsere Loyalität sein. Heil Hitler.' He indicated with his finger the word on the page. 'There, see? It's "Viktoria" not "Sieg".'

'Okay, so they're different words,' said Raye.

'Very different. Viktoria is a feminine proper noun. It's not victory as in something won, it's Victory embodied, like the Roman goddess.'

'The Brandenburg Gate,' said Davis. 'Victory rides a chariot on top of it.'

There was suddenly a tangible energy in the room.

'That's where your plans are,' Duchene said. 'At a Nazi rallying point. He buried it under Victory. Walled up at the Brandenburg Gate.'

Raye was frowning.

'What's the problem?' Duchene said. 'This is good news.'

Raye crossed to the map of Berlin. It now contained marks, notations and coordinates in addition to the pin he'd originally placed to mark Gestapo headquarters.

'The gate is still standing,' Duchene said. 'I saw it when we flew over the city.'

'Not that sort of problem. Here's the gate,' Raye said, marking it with a pin. 'And this line here is the border of the Soviet zone of occupation.' He ran his finger along a black line that divided the city. 'That's problem one.'

The pin lay on the Soviet side of the map.

'Problem two is that the Brandenburg Gate is one of their checkpoints.'

## TWENTY-FIVE

Leterrier shook his head and pointed a thin finger at the map. 'You cannot cross into the Soviet zone.'

'Sirs, if I might speak freely?' Raye said to the assembled officers.

Bennett nodded. 'Go ahead, Captain.'

'I have a way to get into their zone, without being seen. Duchene and I have been there once already. It's discreet. I can get us to the Brandenburg Gate.'

'So, if you were to go, you'd take a team?' Greer asked.

'No sir, I'm suggesting it's just Mr Duchene and myself.'

Leterrier shook his head again. 'Too dangerous. You will cause an international incident if you are caught. Push us closer to conflict. I cannot agree to this.'

'Colonel, sir, it won't be traced back to us. I won't be in uniform. Duchene is a French citizen – he's not even military. This is not a military operation. This is a junior American diplomat and a French translator caught in the wrong place. It's even an advantage that we're from different countries. Met in a bar, got drunk, took a wrong turn. It's not as though they have street signs around here.'

Duchene's discomfort about the plan was growing. He'd remembered their motorbike ride along the Spree and up into Mitte, in and out in less than twenty minutes. This was starting to sound a lot more involved and with less chance of success.

'You know they won't believe that,' Greer said.

'They don't have to believe it. It just needs to be a story they can't disprove. But none of that will happen, I won't get caught.'

'A promise is not a guarantee,' Leterrier said.

Wright ran his fingers along his moustache, then cupped his hand under his chin. 'They should go,' he said. These were his first words since they'd assembled in Raye's office.

'Would you please elaborate?' Bennett asked.

'There's a risk that they'll find nothing. The Brandenburg Gate has survived, yes, but those schematics could be buried under rubble or burnt to ash. If the assessment holds, this Gestapo officer placed the plans in a wall after we stopped our bombing runs, but before the Soviets started to shell the city. There's also the possibility that it's not the plans that are buried there, but something else that this Nazi thinks will incite their resistance. For all we know, it could be Hitler's dentures.'

Leterrier had stopped shaking his head and was listening carefully.

'However,' Wright continued, 'it could be that it *is* the schematics, and the entire purpose of this operation is to keep them from the Soviets. If we do nothing, we risk failing at that. You don't always get to choose the battlefield but you must fight on it nonetheless.'

Bennet shifted in his chair. Above ruddy cheeks, his sharp eyes darted across the faces of the men around him.

'I agree,' said Bennett. 'Colonel, it would be good to make this unanimous.'

Leterrier sighed. 'You force my hand but I agree.'

❧

Three times Duchene prepared himself to stand, to wake Raye and announce that he was no longer willing to risk his life for plans to make new weapons. But each time he arrived at this decision, when the moment came to lever himself out of the cot bed he was lying on, his hands faltered.

Twice now they had averted a direct confrontation – once outside Birgitta Kruger's apartment, the second time at Dr Scheidecker's clinic. Both of those occasions had been in Allied territory. He could imagine the Soviets would be less restrained if it was their borders that had been breached.

This thought drove his fear. Not just for his own safety; he didn't need the call of the void to remind him that he appreciated life. No, there was an overriding fear that they would exchange fire and Sabine would be shot. He saw Sabine falling backwards into the dark, but now she had a bullet through her head. This was no longer about weapons or governments or ideologies. About whether he was a hypocrite, a collaborator, a pacifist or a pawn. None of that mattered. This was all about Sabine. It had always been about Sabine.

It had been too long since he'd slept on anything other than a bed. He'd lost the knack but even if it had still remained, it was unlikely that sleep would have arrived. His mind turned to Sabine and the night to come. So he closed his eyes and let his thoughts continue to churn, as though convincing himself that he was asleep was the next best thing.

About three hours before nightfall, Raye arrived at his side. He was dressed in a black suit and a dark grey shirt. A kind of camouflage that would let him pass as a civilian but also mask his movements at night. He was holding a similar set of clothes for Duchene.

'Time to get ready,' he said. His body was still, loose, relaxed. 'I'll be at the end of the room when you're ready. Don't be long.'

When he rejoined Raye, he was standing at a camp table, checking the slide on a semi-automatic pistol. A private was beside him, putting Allmann's masonry chisel and rock pick in a large satchel.

Raye checked the gun's magazine, chambered one of the bullets and then replaced the missing bullet in the magazine. He held up another pistol – a French Lebel revolver.

'What's this?' asked Duchene.

'Present from Leterrier. Thought you might change your mind about carrying a gun if it was something you were more familiar with.'

Duchene recalled the last time he'd fired one of these. A bad shot, a gut wound. It was enough to slow down a charging German and leave him to bleed to death in the mud as Duchene was pulled back into a trench before another shell erupted earth and stone around him.

He shook his head. 'I thought the goal wasn't to be seen?'

'Sure. But if we are, I want to be able to defend myself.'

Raye tucked a combat knife into the back of his belt, alongside the gun.

'You'll take these,' he said, pointing to identification papers. They were French, diplomatic visas that gave Duchene's actual name and his occupation as translator.

Raye picked up his own papers. 'In case I don't get a chance to defend myself. Let's eat and get ready for the briefing.'

'How are we getting there?'

'Same way as last time.'

'You have another bike?'

Raye smiled. 'The same bike. Another present from Leterrier.'

## TWENTY-SIX

The plan was relatively straightforward. Raye would follow the same rat line along the Spree and into Mitte, into the Soviet zone. In case a show of force was required to deter any Soviet pursuers, a squad of GIs would be stationed at the rat line entrance in Kreuzberg, with a second squad near to the Brandenburg Gate checkpoint. Raye and Duchene would cross the river, emerge into Mitte and wind their way towards Potsdamer Platz, where the Brandenburg Gate was located. They'd leave the bike a block from the gate and cover the last part of the distance on foot.

Just before he and Raye left to lead the GIs' truck into the centre of the city, Duchene visited Corporal Austin in the mess. He was sitting at the end of the table, shovelling food into his mouth from a tin plate as he read.

'Mr Duchene.' He looked up from the Hemingway. 'Thanks again for the book.'

'You're enjoying it?'

'I think I am. It's not a mystery or an adventure, but it's still interesting.'

'That's great.' He held out the basket to the young soldier. 'I was hoping you might –'

'Really?'

'Just hold him for me. For tonight. Unless I don't get back, then he's yours.'

'I'll do that. You can trust him with me.'

Duchene turned to leave.

'Aren't you going to say goodbye to him?' Austin asked.

'He's just a tortoise. He wouldn't understand.'

---

Duchene, like Raye, was wearing goggles as they sped through the night. This brought home the seriousness with which every detail of their safety was being taken. The operation required that they reach their destination without harm and that included a stray insect to the eye.

Raye, too, had changed. A quiet stillness had descended on him. He hadn't even accepted the cigarette that Duchene offered him shortly before their departure. His mind was elsewhere, his thoughts only on the mission.

They reached the ramp that led down to the Spree and Raye swerved into a dark underpass. The sound of the motorcycle echoed around them, intensifying, announcing their presence. Duchene looked over his shoulder at the troop truck as it came to a stop behind them.

They were alone now.

He could smell the river, where plant matter had gathered in tenacious reeds and started to decay. The night was hot and the cool air near the water was a welcome relief. He understood the need for their dark suits, but they reinforced the heat, making it even more oppressive. He could feel the sweat gathering in the small of his back.

Raye pulled the bike up another ramp and turned off its headlight. He slowed to a crawl and began to make his way through the Soviet zone. There was little difference in the landscape – more bombed out buildings, more piles of rubble, more Germans scavenging a living for a future that seemed impossible to imagine. The landscape was the same. What was different was the threat of discovery. Duchene realised that he was gripping the edge of the sidecar to stop his hands from shaking. Even so, small tremors remained. Raye seemed to be feeling the same tension, his shoulders stiff as he hunched over the handlebars, checking the streets around him.

As they drove deeper into Mitte the rubble thinned. Hundreds of thousands of bricks still filled its buildings, but the wide streets were clear and Germans moved about quietly and purposefully, some carrying water back from pumps, others bartering for extra food and blankets.

A patrol of Russian soldiers was walking ahead of them. Raye quickly turned a corner and gradually increased their speed.

'We need to stay on the lit streets,' he said when he was satisfied that they were far enough away. 'Trying to mask our movement in the darkness will only make us look suspicious. Travelling under lights is what a normal Berliner would do.'

'I'm not sure if there's such a thing as normality in Berlin anymore.'

'A fair point. It's also the only way I can follow a map. And we want to keep moving. The longer we're here...' Raye made a wobbling gesture with his hand. 'Not too far now.'

They passed a building that was pristine but for missing glass. Like a lone white horse in the middle of no man's land. Perfect and untouched. But as they turned another corner, the rear of the building came into view – gutted, crumbled and ready to fall.

'Not too far now,' Raye said.

After travelling a few more blocks, Raye made a final turn and cruised up onto the pavement, coming to a stop beside a black pile of debris the size of a small hill. He killed the engine and stepped off the bike.

Once Duchene was out of the sidecar, Raye passed him a torch and removed the satchel. He checked the position of his pistol, then headed for a cleared-out building. Duchene followed him as he moved easily through the entrance doors, their wooden panels scrawled with messages from former residents, parting without resistance. The hallway was almost entirely dark. Only candlelight seeped out from beneath apartment doors, leading them like a runway to the corridor's abrupt end. The back half of the building was missing, as though a giant had simply ripped it away.

Raye took out his map again to study a series of branching red lines that wound their way over the city block. 'This is the best aerial reconnaissance they could provide. We should get a clear run to the edge of Pariser Platz. After that we're going to have to try our luck.'

They climbed carefully down from the edge of the building, then moved on through the ruins. Although the sky was clear, the thin crescent moon offered little help, shedding barely any light on the destruction around them. Duchene stuck close to Raye, trusting in his skill and experience. The American would pause at junctions, kneel and hide his torch under his jacket to check the map before getting up and forging on through the darkness.

After half an hour of careful plotting, they reached the edge of Pariser Platz.

Duchene felt his heart beat faster as he peeked around the corner of a building. The square was vast. On its far side stood the Brandenburg Gate, a blacker silhouette in the darkness, the sculpture a twisted outline. He thought he could just make out the shape of one of the horses and perhaps the raised arm of Victory on the chariot, but it could have just as easily been damaged metal. The wrecked sculpture had taken on a new form, like something out of myth, a chimera. And like a creature of myth it watched over the square, apparently sleeping, but perhaps ready to wake at a moment's notice. The central gap between the huge supporting pillars was wide enough for vehicles to pass through. Attached to the gate on each side, and sharing its covered colonnade, were two neo-classical office buildings, heavily damaged by artillery and gunfire, their edges pocked and shattered.

A female Soviet soldier was standing on a small wooden platform directing traffic. The four temporary streetlights in the dark road afforded just enough visibility so that she could be seen. Her job was largely meaningless; there were no intersections to cross or obstacles to negotiate. Like the huge portrait of Stalin that dominated the centre of the platz, she was a reminder of who now controlled the heart of Berlin.

Duchene said, 'Removing the bricks around the pillars wouldn't be easily done and he would have been seen. It has to be one of those two buildings.'

'Agreed.' Raye was fishing in his pocket. 'But which one?'

'We just have to pick one.'

Raye had removed his deck of cards and was fanning them out to Duchene. 'Red for right. Black for left.'

Duchene extracted a card and turned it over. The six of spades.

'Black swords. Left it is, then,' Raye said. 'Next problem is how to get over there.'

They were beside a large burnt-out hotel, its doors and windows boarded up. In the shadows of a scorched façade Duchene could just make out the name 'Adlon'. On the opposite side stood a line of broken trees growing in ruined grass beds, which continued towards the left-hand administration building. It was otherwise a straightforward route, were it not for the Russians in the centre of the square.

At the base of the gate itself was a wooden boom gate manned by two Russian soldiers, ready to lever it out of the way for any traffic. Like the traffic warden, they were looking away from Duchene and Raye's position, towards their British counterparts on the other side of the official demarcation line. The direction of their focus and the limited illumination might give them a chance of reaching the gate unseen, but success would also put them closer to the guards.

'Can you see the route?' asked Raye.

'Yes,' Duchene replied. 'We follow the wall of the hotel, then move through the trees. Keep to the walls and we'll be in darkness most of the way.'

'It's the noise that will give us away.'

'It's going to make chiselling a wall hard.'

'Agreed. But let's keep it to one complication at a time.'

Raye checked his gun. It was the third time he'd done so since they'd crossed into Mitte. Duchene didn't like the frequency and ease with which Raye reached for the weapon.

They stepped out into the warm breeze that was blowing down the Unter den Linden. With no rubble to hide behind, Raye walked confidently along the outside of the hotel. Beside him, Duchene matched his gait. When they reached the edge of the ornamental tree line they turned left and Raye doubled his pace, crouching low until he reached a pile of rubble. Duchene paused beside him, his heart rate edging up. They were committed now. No more passing themselves off as civilians out for a casual stroll.

'You still with me, old man?'

Duchene nodded.

'Good. You're doing great. Keep close and just follow me.'

Raye set off again, jogging low and navigating the rubble. Duchene made more noise, as broken brick and roof tiles slipped under his feet, but not enough to draw the attention of the Russians. As he bumped and scratched his way towards the building in the darkness, his heart pounding and his hands trembling, Duchene focused on Sabine. She was the only reason he was here. The sooner they found the plans, the safer she would be.

They reached the administration building, Duchene crouching beside Raye in the rubble-filled walkway that separated it from its neighbour. Raye leapt easily over the low, iron fence that surrounded the building; Duchene struggled over, ripping a trouser cuff as he went.

Smaller columns running in a covered colonnade around the building cast darker shadows, giving them a moment to pause.

'Don't die on me,' Raye said, glancing at the wheezing Duchene.

'Let's see how you're going when you're my age.'

'Done. We get through this and in twenty years we'll have a reunion.'

From a blasted window rose the familiar smell of charred wood. Some of the shattered glass still remained in the frame and Raye placed his coat over it. Duchene stepped up onto the sill and lowered himself into the blackness.

Slowly the darkness formed into shapes. They were standing in what had once been an office – they could just glimpse the remains of shelves, perhaps the back of a chair. The floor was covered in ash and charcoal.

'I don't think it's in here,' said Duchene.

'Glad to hear it. Schematics don't tend to last where fire is involved.'

'Think of Allmann's message… If the triumphant weapon is the schematics, heeding the herald of war must mean something as well.'

Duchene moved across the room to look out the window. A car cruised through the columns. The two guards lowered the boom and returned to looking back out towards the British zone beyond them, watching for movement.

From this position he could see the gate's thick outer wall. A brass bowl hung from the ceiling, designed to look like a brazier from antiquity. Below this, in a niche in the wall, was a Roman statue – a figure seated on a cloth-draped plinth, wearing a centurion's helmet and sheathing his sword.

'Mars,' Duchene whispered.

'What have you got?' Raye said, beside him.

'See the alcove and the statue? That's Mars, the god of war.'

'That's it.' Raye could barely stifle his enthusiasm. 'The herald to war.'

'We go out there and we will be a lot closer to those soldiers.'

'Again, these are problems for later.'

A dark red Mercedes-Benz flying two red Soviet flags paused at the gate while the soldiers worked at lifting the boom. Raye tugged on Duchene's arm, and while the men's backs were turned, they scrambled forward through the open doorway, placing their backs against the wall beside the alcove. Around the corner they could hear enthusiastic outbursts of Russian as someone in the car spoke to the guards.

Raye reached a hand around behind the back of the statue. 'Something's been wedged back here. Concreted in.'

He placed his gun on the ground beside him, then removed the rock hammer from the satchel.

'It'll make too much noise,' Duchene whispered.

'The sounds of the car will cover us and I won't hit it hard. Just enough to crack the top. Then I can pull it open.'

The sudden sound of the hammer reverberated through the alcove and up to the ceiling.

Duchene pulled himself sideways and peered over the rubble. The engine grew louder as the big car rolled forward onto Unter den Linden. One guard was pocketing a fresh packet of Marlboros and passing another to his companion.

'Wait,' Duchene whispered. 'Wait for another car.'

Raye, hunched in silence, his hand still on the hammer, gave him a thumbs up.

Duchene pulled his head back as a beam of light swung across the rubble. A large truck, its diesel engine thrumming, was approaching from the opposite direction. By the time it drew up to the boom, the sound was shuddering and echoing around the platz.

Raye's eyes were wild as he hammered several times in quick succession, then used the pick end to lever at the stone behind the plinth. Duchene could see him straining with both hands, before falling backwards. The truck had stopped. The boom was still raised. And then his heart sank.

Out of the cabin stepped Sabine. She tapped the side of the vehicle and a dozen Red Army soldiers leapt down into the square. Unlike the men around her, she wore black knee-high boots and an officer's cap with a bright red band.

'It's Sabine,' Duchene whispered. 'With a truck full of soldiers.'

# TWENTY-SEVEN

Raye wrenched a leather pouch from behind the plinth and snatched up his gun. Duchene, not daring to look over the rubble again, dragged himself across to Raye and pointed back to the office building.

'Through the door, now!' Raye whispered.

Duchene crouched behind Raye as they scrambled towards the door. He felt the air on his back, how exposed he was, blind to what was happening behind him. A fear welled up that every soldier was looking in his direction.

Raye slid into the guardhouse and kicked himself backwards along the floor until he reached the the edge of the door. Duchene came down hard on his knee, driving something sharp between his knee cap and shin. The pain shot through his body and he lost seconds as white pain forced his eyes closed. When he was finally able to open them and scan the square he was briefly relieved to realise that they hadn't been seen.

Raye was looking over at him. 'What happened?'

'Knelt on something.'

Duchene reached down to his knee. Something was sticking out of it. He felt the white pain again, the blood rush from his face and his head roll back as Raye removed a nail from the soft tissue between his bones.

Duchene breathed out carefully. 'Did you get it?'

Raye was smearing ash on his face. 'I got something. Not really the time or the place to check. Can you walk?'

'I think so.'

Duchene pulled himself beside the window as Raye stole another look. 'They're spreading out. We need to keep moving.'

It was easy for Duchene to smear his face: his skin was slick with sweat and his hands were already covered in ash from the floor. Once this was done, he peered over the lip of the window. Just a second was all he got. Just a second was all he needed.

Sabine was standing next to the statue of Mars. In her hand was the rock hammer.

'Fuck,' Raye whispered. 'Now. Move now.'

He grabbed Duchene by the arm and they ran for the window on the opposite site of the room. Raye leapt through it in a single movement, but Duchene had to slow and arrange his weight to compensate for his injured leg. Pain shot through his knee as he staggered back out into the night air.

They fell flat against the wall again. As Raye searched for an escape route, Duchene looked back into the guardhouse. Sabine was approaching it, her hand on her side arm, a torch in her hand. It would be only moments before she'd see their footprints in the ash.

'Does that map of yours have a way out?' he asked.

'Only the way we came in.'

The soldiers had fanned out throughout the square.

'That's not going to work.'

'We need to put some distance between us and the Platz. Then cut across Ebertstrasse We cross that road and we're in the Tiergarten. That's the British zone. We've got our second truck waiting for us there.'

Raye moved along the wrought iron fence and found a gap where falling stone had bent it out of shape. He squeezed through and held out a hand to steady Duchene as he followed.

The adjacent building had been heavily shelled – only three floors remained. Raye ducked into a doorway and re-emerged soon after. 'This way.'

Duchene hobbled after him into the gloom. Filing cabinets had been toppled, their papers scattered. The few desks that remained intact were covered in ceiling plaster. Chairs had been smashed by falling masonry.

'There.' Raye pointed to a window on the opposite wall. 'Through that and out to the Tiergarten.'

He put his arm under Duchene's shoulder. As they neared the window, he could see what the American was referring to. Below them, on the other side of Ebertstasse, were the dark tops of a sea of trees – the Tiergarten. Duchene pushed himself to quicken his pace. They were almost there.

'Don't move.' A woman's voice speaking German.

Sabine.

Raye and Duchene turned.

She was alone, her pistol pointed at them. She frowned as she recognised them, then shook her head and stepped forward to close the distance.

'I told you not to come,' Sabine said in French to Duchene. 'Now look at what you've done.'

She faltered. And that moment was all it took.

In an instant Raye had twisted Duchene's arm and forced him down. Pain ricocheted through his knee as he hit the floor. In the same fluid movement Raye slid behind Duchene and pressed something hard and metallic into the back of his head.

'Comrade Duchene,' Raye said in French. 'Put down the gun or your husband dies.'

# TWENTY-EIGHT

'What are you doing?' Duchene said. Raye was twisting his arm hard at an angle that made it difficult for him to keep his head up and his eyes on Sabine.

'You're bluffing,' she said to Raye.

'But how can you be sure? You know nothing about me, Sabine, and I know so much more about you.' Something new had entered Raye's voice – an icy calmness.

'You've kept him alive these last three days. You're allies, on the same side. You're not going to kill him.' Somehow Sabine had matched him, her voice free of emotion or emphasis. Neither seemed to be bluffing.

'He's only here because you're leading the Soviet team. That's the only reason he's in Berlin.'

'You needed him to find those plans.'

'I needed him because he's your husband and you won't want to see him harmed. He's only here for precisely such a moment as this.'

'That's not true.'

'Drop the gun.'

Duchene hoped she was right. He wanted her to be right. It

made no sense that Raye would actually be threatening his life. Not now. Not after he'd brought them here, found the schematics. Then again, this was a man fighting a war. His enemy might have changed and the battlegrounds become covert, but it was still a war and wars made men brutal and desperate.

Raye spoke again. 'Drop the gun.'

He let go of Duchene's arm and pulled back the slide of the semi-automatic revolver. It ejected the pre-loaded round, spinning it through the air and off a spilt filing cabinet. This slid a new round into the chamber, resetting the firing mechanism. It was completely unnecessary, but completely underlined his point.

Duchene watched as Sabine turned her gun sideways and moved her finger away from the trigger. Metal scraped on metal as she stepped forward and placed the gun on the top of a cabinet, then raised her hands. Through the window behind her there was movement. The soldiers were getting closer.

'Good,' Raye said. 'Now step back.'

Duchene barely had time to react in the seconds before it happened. The movement he had glimpsed was much closer than he'd first realised. As a soldier stepped into view, held his rifle at his hip and fired at Raye, Duchene did the only thing he could do – rammed Raye forwards, out of the firing line. The shot went wide and filled the room with noise.

Sabine lunged for the gun but not before Raye kicked over the cabinet, sending the gun to the floor and the drawers towards her. Sabine moved aside to avoid being hit, but in doing so came nearer to Raye. He grabbed her around the neck, choking her as his arm tightened. She stamped down hard on his foot, causing

Raye to wince, but failing to deter him from bringing the pistol to her head.

There were shouts from outside and the sound of running boots. Another soldier appeared at the window beside the first shooter. Raye fired a shot towards them, the crack of the pistol so close to her ear causing Sabine to flinch in pain. The soldiers ducked back behind cover.

'Tell them to stay back,' Raye shouted in French.

By now Duchene had crawled across the floor and was crouched behind a toppled cabinet.

'Tell them!' Raye shouted.

'Ne strelyay!' Sabine shouted. 'Ne. Strelyay.'

'No what?' Raye demanded. 'You said "no" what? "Surrender"?'

'I said "no shooting".'

'Raye! She said the same thing the other day when we were on the motorbike,' Duchene said. He could see more movement behind them, at the window looking out over the Tiergarten.

'Fuck!' Evidently Raye had seen the same thing. He looked towards the stairs that led up to the next floor. They were mostly intact.

'Up. Next floor. Now! Auguste, can you see her gun?' Raye kept his arm around Sabine and hustled her towards the stairs.

'You just had a gun at my head,' said Duchene. 'You want me to give you a second one?'

'I wasn't going to shoot you.'

'I knew it,' Sabine growled.

'But yes, I did use you. If we get out of here we can hash it out then. Just grab her gun.'

Duchene pushed aside some of the papers to find her pistol. It was completely cast out of metal and on its grip was stamped the Soviet star. He picked it up. It was a heavy, brutal thing.

Raye shoved Sabine up the stairs and Duchene followed.

The second storey of the damaged office building was almost identical to the ground floor, its only point of difference lying above them. The ceiling bulged under the weight of the upper floors that had collapsed on it. Spiderwebbed across it were large fissures and cracks – the whole thing was ready to split.

Raye pushed Sabine into a chair, then began to tie her to it, using his belt.

'Is that necessary?' Duchene asked.

'She's an enemy combatant,' Raye said, threading the belt between the back of the chair and around her wrists. 'I can't just let her walk about.'

Duchene turned to Sabine. 'Can't you order them to let us go?'

'I can't. I won't.' Sabine replied in the same emotionless tone.

'Gun,' Raye said, holding his hand out to Duchene.

Duchene handed it over.

With Sabine's pistol in his left hand, and his own weapon in the other, Raye edged a look back down the staircase. He fired off a shot from each pistol. 'I told you to tell them to fall back,' Raye said.

'I told them not to shoot,' Sabine said. 'There's a difference.'

Raye dragged a cabinet to the edge of the stairs and kicked it over. Duchene could hear it slamming down, its drawers falling free.

'What if we give you the schematics?' he said. 'Will you call them off then? Let us go?'

'Yes. But you'll want to do that quickly. My men will have called for reinforcements by now. In the next five minutes this place will be swarming with Red Army soldiers and someone more senior than me will be giving the orders.'

Duchene couldn't understand how she and Raye were able to keep thinking and talking. He felt numbed by the chaos around him, the threat of being shot, the thought of being captured, of living a short, brutal life in a gulag.

Raye was heaving another cabinet towards the stairs. 'Don't be a fucking traitor, Duchene. I'll do my best to pretend you never said that.'

'I can't let you go without something to show for it,' said Sabine. 'The NKVD will have me executed – also as a traitor. So it's either hand me the plans or shoot me now.'

Raye kicked the second cabinet down the stairwell.

He turned to Sabine. 'Five minutes, you say?'

He grabbed her right hand. She tried to keep her fist closed but he forced it open.

'Stop!' Duchene shouted. 'What are you doing?'

He limped across the room but didn't make it. Raye pulled back her right ring finger and snapped it.

Sabine screamed – part pain, part anger – her voice breaking from her mouth in a roar. 'Fuck you!'

'Right, the next one then.'

Duchene seized Raye's arm. 'Stop!'

Then, before he had time to register what was happening, Raye had grasped him by the lapels and thrown him backwards. Duchene staggered, his right knee jarring as he crashed into the side of a desk.

Raye returned to Sabine and snapped another finger. She screamed. Tears were flooding her face, she was gasping.

Duchene tried to stop his voice from faltering, to speak calmly as he fought against his racing heart and mind. 'Louis. Please. Don't do this.'

'She'll break. She'll give them the order to step down. We're almost out of here.' Raye's voice was toneless but there was desperation in his eyes.

'Stop hurting her!'

'Then convince her! You tell your wife to do what she's told.'

'I can't. She won't listen to me. Not when she's made up her mind. She never has.'

'No? Fine. Then I move to the next stage.'

Raye pulled his knife from his belt and raised it over her leg.

A gunshot cracked around them. Raye stumbled backwards. He stared at Duchene, his eyes wide, confused. Not afraid, but indignant. Blood was spreading, dark red on the front of his grey shirt, spilling from the side of his mouth.

Duchene didn't understand either. He turned to see if a soldier was standing behind him. Nothing. Sabine was staring at him. At the pistol he held in his hand.

He threw it back onto the table. 'I –'

'You shot him,' she said, watching as the knife that just seconds earlier had been about to stab her leg, fell from Raye's hand.

'I didn't –'

'You did. Quick, get me out of here.'

Duchene felt faint, his stomach churning, his chest tightening with pain. The room began to spin around him, his eyes didn't know where to focus.

'Auguste!'

He shook his head, tried to take a deep breath.

'Just walk towards me. Give me your belt.'

He listened to her voice, let it draw him to her. The room was still spinning but it was starting to slow. He fumbled with the belt buckle, tugged it, pulled it free.

Sabine burst up and grabbed the gun from the table. Her eyes were fixed on the stairwell.

She fired two wild shots down the stairwell with her left hand.

Duchene shook his head. 'What's happening?'

She shook him by the shoulders. 'Auguste, we have seconds if we're lucky. I need you with me now. Here. Now. With your wife.'

The fog was lifting from his head.

'I shot him.'

'Forget that.' She spoke through gritted teeth as she fed one belt through the buckle of the other one to link them. Her broken fingers were now fat and swollen. 'You need to get out of that window. Can you handle a drop?'

'I think I –'

'Good. Take the plans. Go back to the west.'

'You take them. What are you going to tell the NKDV?'

'NKVD. Give me that gun.' She pointed to the Russian pistol he was holding.

She sent another three bullets from Raye's gun down the stairwell before dropping the weapon beside his body. His blood was pooling on the floor.

'I've just killed an enemy agent in our territory. That's something I can use. It should be enough.' She passed Duchene the schematics. 'You need to take something back to the Americans.

That will help them to accept this man's death had a purpose. It means they won't look at you closely. They'll blame it on us.'

He began to object. 'Auguste, I'm telling you. This is how we will both survive this. How we will both stay alive.' She led him over to the window.

'I don't want you to leave. Come with me.'

'I do that and they'll have me assassinated. I was wrong. What I said before.' She checked the ground beneath the window. 'We're not completely different. We do have something in common: we're survivors. We learn and we adapt and we survive. Survive this night with me now and one day we might meet again. Yes?'

'Yes.'

'Good. I'm going to call for them. As soon as those men have moved away from the window, I need you to climb out and then drop. We have to get the timing right. Don't hit the ground until they've breached the building.'

Duchene placed his good leg on the edge of the frame, then reached into his pocket. 'Here,' he said, holding out her wedding ring. 'In case you still want this?'

She smiled briefly as a tear rolled from her eye. 'Top pocket.'

He slipped it into her uniform.

'Soldat! Na moyu pozitsiyu!' Her voice rang out in the night air. 'Na moyu pozitsiyu!'

Duchene clambered out, the soles of his shoes slipping on the wall until he managed to tuck his feet into a hole a couple of metres below the window. He then moved his arms down the strap. His hands were sweating. It was hard to hold.

Sabine was leaning her body weight away from him, her face red. She was gritting her teeth again, the belt wrapped around her right arm while her damaged hand only partly gripped the leather.

'Now,' she said, her voice hoarse, passing from her with what little strength she had remaining.

Duchene looked to the rubble below, saw a clear space and jumped. As he hit the ground, white-hot pain shot through his right leg, which spasmed beneath him. Looking up, he saw Sabine nod, acknowledging that he'd landed. She dropped the makeshift rope down to him. He caught it, but when he looked back up, she had disappeared.

He could hear Sabine's voice echo in the room above, shouting orders in Russian.

Duchene hobbled along the wall and slid into the blast crater from an exploded shell. He craned his neck back towards the building as he freed his belt and replaced it around his waist. He could hear the rumble of more trucks arriving at the Brandenburg Gate, filling the air with the smell of their diesel. He peered over the edge of the crater. Torchlight was flickering from the building above him. Now came the sound of boots on stone, echoing through the square. He checked to see that the document pouch was secure over his shoulder.

With each step an agony, he clambered get out of the crater and started to slide down the embankment. Dry soil was everywhere – in his clothes, on his face, in his mouth. He stopped and leant against a wrecked German truck that had been dragged to the side of the street. The smell of burnt metal lingered around it – the ghost of flame.

The shouting behind him was growing louder, the torches were getting nearer.

He looked out towards the darkness of the Tiergarten. It was large, easy to get lost in, but also better for not being discovered. He couldn't make out the Victory Column in the centre of the forest. Without Raye, without his map, he couldn't be sure he'd find their reserve truck. He was even less confident that his leg would support him that distance.

The alternative was to follow the edge of the park north, towards the opposite side of the Brandenburg Gate. There would have to be an Allied checkpoint there. If he could reach it, and if the soldiers manning it could hold their ground, there might be a way to make it through the night.

But this would mean crossing the brightly lit no man's land of Ebertstrasse. A short width of road that might as well be an endless desert. To cross it would risk his life. But if he were to stay, he'd get caught, be interrogated by the NKVD, risk Sabine's life and squander what she had done to save him.

He breathed in and started to run, pushing his legs to move as fast as they would let him. He was out into the road and halfway across before the shooting started.

At first it was a single shot, the sound of a bullet rushing past his ear. He was going over the top of the trenches again, as the men under his command fell lifeless around him. But not running into a storm of lead. No, not this time. Now he was running away as, like the slow build of a rain shower, a second, third and then a fourth shot rang out.

Duchene pushed himself harder, each step like a new hammer blow, a fresh puncture to his knee.

He hit the tree line and burst through it, stumbling over rough ground. His momentum was too much – he tripped and sprawled onto the grass. His lungs were heaving. His limbs trembled. His entire body was slicked with sweat.

From behind him the firing had stopped. He heard the shrill of a whistle. Sending men forward or calling them back.

He pulled himself up and strained through the darkness of the park towards the lights at the Soviet checkpoint outside the Brandenburg Gate. Turning his gaze to the west, he saw its Allied counterpart. Only fifty metres from the Soviets but, as far as he was concerned, half a continent away.

He could hear feet pounding on the Ebertstrasse behind him. Duchene ran again, his eyes fixed on the Allied checkpoint. It became all he could see, all he could think of, as his peripheral vision began to blur. A dreadful numbness was moving through his injured leg; his foot seemed to land more awkwardly with each new step.

He burst out of the trees.

The stunned expressions on the faces of the British soldiers quickly shifted to frowns of anger and alarm. They raised their rifles.

'Don't shoot,' he shouted in English. 'My name is Auguste Duchene. I'm a French citizen. I have classified information for Brigadier Thomas Wright.'

A sergeant grabbed him by the collar and pulled him past the line that had formed of half a dozen soldiers. They stood their ground as the Russians emerged from the trees. As both sides started shouting, in their own languages, Duchene slumped down against some sandbags. He tightened his grip on the document pouch and passed out.

## Monday, 6 August 1945

# TWENTY-NINE

A light rain began to fall, breaking the heat, bringing respite to parched soil and quelling the dust. Duchene couldn't appreciate any of this. Not yet. He was sitting up in a hospital bed in an infirmary at Andrews Barracks. The heat from the night still lingered in here, and until the windows were opened, or the rain increased, it would take time for the cool change to reach him.

He remembered very little of how he had got to the ward, only snatches of memory that he'd tried to wrangle into order. Strapped to a stretcher in the back of a swaying truck. A young medic looking down at him. The bright lights of an operating theatre, a dressing being placed on his leg.

A young nurse was checking on her patients. There were six beds in the room, three facing three, but only four were occupied. She reminded him a little of Marienne – her smile, the dark hair. She was carrying a clipboard and making notes after referring to the charts at the foot of each bed.

She reached his chart and started to review it.

'I've forgotten my English,' Duchene said to her.

'Sounds as though you're speaking it quite well, Mr Duchene.'

'No. I need a word. A specific word,' he replied. 'What's my prognostic?'

'You mean "prognosis". But that's not the word you're after. You mean "diagnosis".'

'Ah.'

She smiled. 'You're going to be fine. You've managed to puncture the meniscus in your knee. The doctor thinks it's torn, but he'll need to take another look when the swelling has gone down. You've been given an anti-tetanus injection just in case.'

'From the nail?'

'It's all you could talk about when they brought you in. The medic did the right thing and gave you a syrette of morphine, but it took a little while before we could put our finger on exactly what had happened.'

'And my ankle?' He had noticed the support bandage around it.

'Torn ligament. You'll need crutches for a few weeks. You'll have to keep off that right leg altogether.'

Duchene lay back. 'Thank you.'

---

He woke again, later in the morning. Or did he come to? He couldn't remember if he'd fallen asleep or passed out.

The rain was falling harder now and the cool air had finally entered the room. Corporal Austin was sitting beside him.

'How long have you been there?'

'Not long, sir.'

'Auguste. You can call me Auguste.'

'I was sent to work out a way to bring you to Major General Bennett. They're wanting a debriefing. And I thought you might like to see him?' Austin nodded towards the basket at his feet.

'He's still alive and happy?'

'Yes. Of course.'

'Then I don't need to see him. Although if I'm going to be here for a few days, I might need you to keep looking after him.'

He sat up straighter. There was bone weariness now on top of the pain. 'Have to smarten up if I'm going to meet a general.'

As he got dressed, he felt as though he was moving through water. Each limb seemed to encounter an invisible resistance, slowing his movements, disrupting his coordination. It was only stubbornness and a refusal to accept the weakness of his own body that meant he finally emerged from the curtains around his bed. He turned down Austin's offer of a wheelchair, instead hobbling on crutches along the white tiles of the infirmary and out into the rain.

It was refreshing in the brief moment that it fell on his skin before Austin opened an umbrella above his head. As they made their way slowly towards the administration building, Duchene recommended some new titles for the corporal to read next – *The Grapes of Wrath* and Conrad's *The Secret Agent*.

With Austin beside him, Duchene made his way down the long hallway that bisected the main foyer and led to Bennett's office. As they were passing the wide staircase that went up to the second and third storeys, he heard his name being called.

First Sergeant Davis was part way up, each foot on different step, talking to a red-headed clerk. She cut short the conversation and came quickly down to meet him.

'Monsieur Duchene, I just wanted to be the first to say, I'm sorry about Captain Raye.'

'That's, uh, good of you. Thank you.'

He started to move on and Davis followed. 'I know you didn't know him for all that long, but I also know how he had this way of making an impression.'

*The crack of bone as a finger was snapped.*

'Yes, he did. I'm sorry he didn't make it.' Duchene stopped. 'Actually I was hoping you might be able to help me with something. Things are a little hazy. They had me on morphine. What did I report last night? About Raye. How did he die?'

Davis turned to Austin. 'Corporal, please give us a moment.'

When the young man was out of earshot Davis looked around nervously. 'I'm not supposed to say.'

'Even though I gave a report?'

'You provided some information for a larger report. There's sensitive information in there.'

'Such as the agent we have working for us within the Soviets? Who their handler is?'

Davis stepped closer and whispered into his ear. 'You're not really supposed to know about that. Look, all you said was that Raye had been shot in Mitte. You refused to say who killed him.'

'Am I going into a briefing or an interrogation?'

'Monsieur Duchene…'

'Sergeant, I almost died out there. For your country. I'm just asking for you to steer me in the right direction.'

'They'll want to ask you some questions. Yes.'

'Pointed questions?'

A nod.

'And the schematics?'

She shook her head. 'Better that you talk to them about that.'

'Alright. Thank you for the advice.'

'Good luck, Monsieur Duchene.'

Austin returned to his side and they resumed their journey towards the office. The door was opened almost as soon as he knocked, by Bennett himself. He dismissed Austin and quickly ushered Duchene inside and into a chair. Leterrier stood and shook Duchene's hand while Wright, still seated, tipped a lethargic hand to his head. Greer was staring out the window.

'Well done, Mr Duchene,' said Bennett as he placed a decanter on the coffee table where five whisky tumblers were waiting. 'Some of us were sceptical, but the late Captain Raye was convinced you were the right person for this operation. Looks like he was right, God rest his soul.'

'I'm sorry that he died,' Duchene said, looking at Greer.

The major turned back to the room. 'He was a good soldier. A good man.'

*The knife about to plunge into Sabine's leg.*

'It is a loss to the service.' Bennett removed the top from the decanter. 'But a day to celebrate.' Large slugs of liquor hit the bottom of each glass in turn. 'We're on the cusp of bringing this war to the end.'

'And the schematics?' Duchene asked. 'I never got to see them. They were what you were after?'

'Yes,' said Greer without emotion. 'Exactly what we were hoping for.'

'They're not in the hands of the Soviets, so it will delay them a little longer,' said Bennett.

'From building rockets of their own?' Duchene asked.

Leterrier looked at the faces of the men around him.

'From building nuclear rockets of their own,' Wright said.

Bennett spoke again. 'But after today, the Soviets will know we're serious. And that's what we're here to toast.'

'We're drinking to the schematics being kept out of their hands?' Duchene asked.

Leterrier smiled while Bennett laughed.

'Not exactly,' Wright said, smirking. 'Just this morning the Americans have emphasised how serious we are about bringing the war with Japan to an end.'

'I'm not following.'

'You won't.' Geer strolled across to the table and picked up a glass. 'In the next few hours, you will.'

'I'm sorry, Mr Duchene,' Bennett said. 'Just a bit of bonhomie. That's French, right?'

'Different word,' Leterrier said.

'To the end of the war,' Bennett said and raised his glass.

Everyone took measured sips but Greer, who finished his drink in one hit.

Bennett's eyes narrowed, but he said nothing.

'Can you tell us what happened?' Leterrier asked. 'To Captain Raye?'

Duchene replaced his glass on the table and put his hands on the arms of the chair.

'We found the schematics, hidden by Allmann in an alcove at the base of the Brandenburg Gate. But as we were leaving, the Russian team arrived, with about a dozen soldiers. I didn't get the numbers exactly. Raye and I retreated to a bombed building. Our goal was to get to the Tiergarten and meet up with the American truck at the Victory Column.

'But the Russians saw us, started firing on our position. Raye gave me the schematics and told me to run while he provided covering fire. As I was climbing out of the building he was shot. I ran to the nearest Allied soldiers, the British at the Ebertstrasse checkpoint.'

'You're saying Raye sacrificed himself so that you could escape?' Greer asked. He had remained standing and was gripping his empty glass so tightly that his knuckles were turning white.

Because Duchene's stomach was empty, the alcohol was moving quickly through his system, hitting the painkillers and playing with his mind. 'I don't think that's what he'd planned. He wanted to draw their fire so I had time to get across to the park, then he would follow. My leg was injured and we both knew he would be able to move faster. He was better than me at moving through the rubble.'

'Huh,' Greer grunted and returned to the window.

Wright watched him from the corner of his eye. 'Did you recognise any of the Russians in the team that was firing on Raye?'

'Well, my wife was there, if that's what you're asking.'

'Was she the one who gave the order to fire?'

'No. A second and third truck arrived. Those were the teams that started shooting.'

'Three trucks?' Greer asked. 'I thought you said it was one?'

The room was silent. A specific quiet when bodies hold themselves still and slow their breathing. He could see now where the questions were leading – they were trying to catch him out, steer him into a lie.

'Yes. You'll have to forgive me if I don't have all my thoughts in order. They gave me morphine last night. My memory is still catching up.'

Leterrier placed his elbows on his knees. 'Why do you think your wife didn't give the order to fire?'

Defensive answers weren't working. It was time to change tack.

'The answer is already in your question. She is my wife. Captain Raye explained that was the reason I was on the operation – to discourage her from firing on or capturing us. And to provide advice about what she might be thinking.'

'He told you this?' Wright asked.

'It does sound like Raye,' Bennett said, taking another sip of Scotch.

'That's what made him good at what he did,' said Greer.

*The air filling with the smell of burnt metal as the bullet struck Raye in the chest.*

'He saved my life,' Duchene said.

Greer spoke from the window, his eyes on the floor. 'The armourer said that you refused a Lebel revolver when you were preparing to leave on the operation.'

'That's right.'

'Was there a specific reason you went in unarmed?'

'I had understood we were trying to avoid an international incident.'

'So you didn't handle a gun during the whole operation?'

'I did. At one point Raye passed me his pistol.'

'But you didn't fire it?' Greer's hands were gripping the edge of the sill.

Bennett and Leterrier turned their full attention to Duchene. Wright, too, was watching him, waiting for his answer.

'No. Is there a problem, gentlemen?'

They remained silent.

'No.' Bennett clapped his hands on his knees and smiled. 'No problem at all.' He stood and reached out a hand. 'Well, Mr Duchene, thank you very much for your service. It's a shame you didn't re-enlist or there'd probably be a medal in this for you. Isn't that right, Colonel?'

Leterrier grimaced. 'Probably.'

Duchene shook Bennett's hand as Wright and Leterrier rose from their seats. The signal had been given. It was time to go.

Duchene stood and pulled his crutches under his arms. He shook each man's hand in turn.

'My pleasure. Glad I could help.'

Bennett saw him out. 'I understand that Dr Patterson is keen to keep you under observation for another day or two. You are, of course, welcome here on base. If we have any further questions, we'll have someone bring you over.'

Duchene thanked him.

The general closed the door.

# THIRTY

Duchene slowly opened his eyes. The ward was full of the heavy smell of disinfectant. Outside, crickets sang in the heat of the night.

'I'm sorry to wake you,' the nurse whispered, 'but you have a visitor.'

He pushed himself up from the bed, looked outside. Lights around the camp pinpointed key locations: the guardhouses, the duty office of the administration building, the barracks.

'What time is it?'

'It's 11 p.m.'

'You can bring them in.'

'Actually, they want you to go to them. Outside.'

Duchene pulled on a dressing gown, slipped a shoe onto his left foot and steadied himself on his crutches before following the nurse, who held the door for him as he stepped outside.

He could smell the cigarette smoke before he saw the figure sitting on the fresh pine bleachers of a new baseball field. The man wore an officer's cap, but in the darkness Duchene couldn't identify the army, let alone the rank.

He hobbled towards the figure, who was leaning back against

a bleacher. In one hand was a cigarette, in the other a small hip flask.

Duchene didn't need to see his face to know who it was.

'Bloyer.'

The Frenchman stood and turned to face Duchene. 'Monsieur, it's been a while.'

The effects of the morphine had worn off and Duchene's mind was feeling whole again. The sparks were there, letting him make the leaps he was used to, that he so often relied on.

'You're the one with the Soviet informant. The person Raye's been calling for information.'

'Glad to see you haven't changed.' Bloyer tapped the side of his head. 'Still a good thinker. Please sit.'

Bloyer shuffled down the bleacher and repositioned himself. 'I hope you're not too badly injured,' he said, reaching out to take the crutches.

Duchene let him do so, but left some distance between himself and the other man.

'Cigarette?' Bloyer held out a packet of Gauloises.

'I have my own.' Duchene lit a Lucky Strike.

'Our friends the Americans have had their influence on you already. Can't get by without the comforts of their own home. What is this field for? One of their games, no?'

'Baseball.'

'Ah, yes. Baseball...'

Bloyer unscrewed the top of the hip flask and held it out to Duchene. 'Brandy?'

He shook his head.

Bloyer shrugged and took a sip. 'I was sorry to hear Raye died.'

'I was sorry to be there when it happened.'

'He was a good soldier, a good intelligence officer.'

'And you?'

'Am I a good soldier?'

'Military intelligence? I assume that's what you are if you have an informant.'

'Yes. I'm with the BCRA,' said Bloyer

'Ah, more acronyms.'

'I think it's intended to confound the enemy.'

'You disappeared at the start of the war.'

'I re-enlisted,' Bloyer replied. 'Unlike you. I did tell them you'd never do it. Not sure if I'm glad to see I was right.'

'So what about the party? Those murders didn't get you what you were after, so you changed sides?'

'Now that's something I thought we had in common. Pragmatism. No, I *know* we have it in common. I saw through the mystique, the truth at the heart of Stalin. The assassination of the enemies of communism, the battle against counter-revolutionaries... It made sense, but not when I saw the scale, not when I learnt the truth of the purges, of the massacres, the millions of Ukrainians who starved. The non-aggression pact with the Nazis was the final straw. Our leaders have still failed Poland, even now...'

'Bullshit.'

Bloyer laughed. 'That's right. Sabine always said you didn't understand idealism.'

'Why are you here?'

'I want to help you. And Sabine.'

'Why?'

'Because of where the world stands, Monsieur Duchene. This morning the Americans dropped an atomic bomb on Japan. We have limited information, but we know this place, Hiroshima, was flattened. Just one bomb. More power than twenty thousand tonnes of TNT. Eighty per cent of the city was flattened. Your race against Sabine wasn't the only one being run…' He drew on his cigarette and let the smoke curl from his mouth. 'The next war has already started, even before the last one has ended and our new enemy are the Soviets.'

'How does that help me or Sabine?'

'Because she's trapped. She might not know it yet, but I think she does. The NKVD are quick to arrest, even quicker to execute. She needs to move with caution. Even as a high-ranking officer she will never be completely safe. In Russia there's only loyalty to Stalinist policy. Clearly your wife is torn. And that will eventually make her a target.'

'Is she safe?'

'For now. My informant can't be everywhere. Their knowledge is limited. But Comrade Major Dubovoya's mission has been construed as a successful one. An attempt to infiltrate the Soviet zone by enemy agents was thwarted. The Brandenburg Gate was thoroughly searched and the schematics they were after had been destroyed days before the Red Army even reached Berlin.'

'And what about me? I escaped.'

'You were "incorrectly identified". Just a Berliner who almost got shot. A good example of the restraint and tolerance of Soviet soldiers.'

'Why do you want to get her out of Soviet Berlin?'

'You're a clever man, so I won't try to dress this up –'

Duchene cut across him. 'She's Soviet military intelligence. She'll have information for the Allies.'

'Exactly. But you get to know that she's safe again. Both of you can carry on with your lives.'

Duchene's cigarette was long with ash. He tapped it off and inhaled.

'Except the NKVD won't let that pass – surely. They'll go hunting for her. Like they did with Trotsky.'

'Perhaps. But we can take steps to hide her. The truth is, Monsieur, Sabine is on borrowed time. She's clever. She can last for a while. But she won't survive indefinitely. Better to have her here in the west than remain in the east under threat. I can promise you, this conflict with the Soviets, their suspicion, ours, will only get worse. Trust is a scarce commodity these days.'

'Well put. So why should I trust you?'

'Oh, you should absolutely trust no one. But you should still make deals.' Bloyer took another sip from the flask and waved it in Duchene's direction.

This time he took it.

'You see,' said Bloyer. 'You don't have to trust me to get something out of our conversation. Your friends this afternoon didn't trust you. Even after everything you'd done for them.'

'Greer, Bennett, Wright?'

'And our esteemed Colonel Leterrier too. You mustn't forget him.'

'What do you mean?'

'While you were incapacitated, doped up on morphine, you told the medic you killed Raye.'

'That's strange because I'm not doped up now, and I can tell you I didn't kill him.'

Bloyer laughed. 'Very good. See. You're learning fast. That's one of the things that's always impressed me about you.'

'What are they going to do?'

'Well, you haven't confessed to anything and you're a French citizen. Handing you over to the Americans to prosecute won't improve their relationship with General de Beauchesne, who heads the French forces in Berlin. My understanding is that Greer is the only one who's looking for retribution. Which won't be forthcoming if you agree to my offer.'

'Don't trust, but make deals…'

'Exactly. It may not seem like it, but Leterrier was impressed with your performance. We're asking you again to re-enlist. To stay here in Berlin. To use your cleverness to help us avoid a full-blown war with the Soviets.'

'Avoid a war or help start one?'

Bloyer frowned. 'It won't be long before they have atomic bombs of their own, inside rockets. We all will. And no one wants a war then.'

Duchene picked up his crutches and got to his feet.

'I've offended you?'

'No. I've heard what you have to offer.' He gingerly took a couple of tender steps onto the baseball field.

'And?'

And he and Sabine were trapped by their pasts. Not just the choices they'd made to survive the war, the sides they'd chosen, but the ways in which they'd kept themselves alive. Perhaps he would never see Sabine again, perhaps they would never get the chance to forge a new life together. But, as she had said, they were both survivors, and if they both held true to her belief, then maybe they could find a way.

## ACKNOWLEDGEMENTS

This book was written on the unceded lands of the Woi Wurrung and Boon Wurrung people of the Eastern Kulin nations, and the author pays his respects to their Elders, past, present and emerging. Always was, always will be Aboriginal land.

I want to thank my publishers, Juliet Rogers and Diana Hill, for your belief, enthusiasm and commitment to continuing Duchene's story. This book exists because of you.

I am grateful to my editor, Anna Rogers, whose guidance and insight have been invaluable. Your many hours of feedback and considered analysis turned a manuscript into a novel. Thank you also to Debra Billson for another stunning cover that captures so much of what this novel is about. As always, I am indebted to my agent Fiona Inglis for her advice and representation.

Thank you to Ben Chessell for your generous insights and the benefit of your experience. To my family, Carol-Anne, Terence and Claire, for supporting and travelling with me through my writing journey. To Patrick O'Shea for always being the first reader. And to Francesca and Genevieve, my daughters, for your boundless optimism about my work, even if you're still too young to read it.

Finally, to my wife Berni, to whom this book is dedicated, you helped to shape it in many ways. Your belief and encouragement make all the difference. You are forever my inspiration.

# The first Auguste Duchene novel – *The Paris Collaborator*

August, 1944. In German-occupied Paris, former schoolteacher Auguste Duchene has stumbled upon an unusual way to survive: he finds missing people. When he's approached by members of the French Resistance to locate a missing priest – and a cache of stolen weapons – Duchene initially refuses. But the Resistance offer him no choice. Within hours, he's also blackmailed by a powerful Nazi into searching for a German soldier who's suspected of deserting.

To fail at either task will have deadly consequences for Duchene – and for his daughter Marienne.

So begins a frantic race against time. As forces close in on Paris, Duchene has only 48 hours to locate the missing priest and the missing soldier, or lose the only person he loves…